PHANTOM MARAUDERS

OF THE BERMUDA TRIANGLE

by R.C. Farrington

Illustrated by Jason Farrington

This war on drugs will take no prisoners.

ISBN: 1-4662-4092-X
ISBN-13: 978-1-4662-4092-6

www.bermudaspinners.com

WONDERFUL PEOPLE WHO CONTRIBUTED TO THIS BOOK:

Jason Farrington has created outstanding graphic designs for this novel.
www.gorilladesignstudio.net

Rod Ferguson of Bermuda and Pat Farrington of the United States
have made contributions of their time and thoughts to help
make this novel possible.

I would also like to extend a special thank you to Delta Air Lines for all
the smooth trips and outstanding flight crews on my many flights to and
from Bermuda. Because of this I was able to write many pages of this
novel while in the air with Delta.

DEDICATION:

I would like to dedicate this novel to a drug free world. Although the backdrop of this novel is in Bermuda, the reality is that it could be anywhere in the world. The war on drugs is not isolated to any single location, nor is there a single solution for its eradication. Only the perseverance and dedication of concerned citizens and law enforcement agencies will bring this epidemic to an end. Education of our youth about the pitfalls of drug addiction is important, but equally important is a quality of overall education that will allow our youth to become productive participants in the communities they live in without resorting to drugs. Those with addictions must also have a chance to recover from their hopelessness in order to discover a life without dependencies.

The future can be bright for all of us, but the war on drugs and the illegal weapons they also bring is far from over. We must not become complacent and expect others to fight this battle while we sit idly on the sidelines. No matter who we are, we must unite in this war together. The future generations of our planet are depending on what we do today.

This novel depicts an aggressive unorthodox battle strategy for the war on drugs. Cut off the head of the serpent.

INTRODUCTION:

Bermuda is the most beautiful place on earth, and whoever reads this novel should take at least one week out of their busy lives to visit one of the most incredible places on the earth. There you will find soft pristine turquoise-colored waves gently rolling up on the pink beaches. You will also find breathtaking the myriad combinations of arbors, shrubs, vines and flowers that reflect all the colors of the rainbow. Then, when you consider the historic Forts, the village of St. George's and the most picturesque golf courses in the world..... Yes, Bermuda is truly an island paradise.

CHAPTERS:

CHAPTER 1

Lost and Found

LOST AND FOUND

'The Rusty Bucket', an old converted tug boat had been out scouring the waters in the vast Bermuda Triangle for weeks. The skipper of the tug was Turk Black, a light skinned Bermudian about six feet one inches tall with a medium muscular build. Turk had lived a tough life, and his face showed the effects of stress, the sun, and the salt air. Even though he'd seen and done about everything, he was still able to handle whatever life threw at him. Occasionally, someone would notice his glass eye in his right socket. This scar was from a fight he was in years ago when a drug bust went bad. Because of the discomfort of the glass eye, he usually wore a black eye patch whenever he was on the open seas; even though his crew gave him a hard time about it.

The lifestyle of a professional salvage and treasure hunter had suited him well. Now with the downturn of the current economy, he had been desperately trying to find a lost deserted ship in the waters of the Bermuda Triangle. Having the salvage rights for a ship was better than finding lost treasure. Turk's first mate Bucko was at the helm of the tug while he was standing at the bow scanning the horizon with his monocular for anything of interest. As he leaned over the railing Turk's thoughts drifted back to his past. Although he had been in the salvage and treasure hunting business for three years his roots were really in the law enforcement business. For almost seven years, Turk had been one of the best undercover narcotic officers in Bermuda. He regretted leaving the police force, but Bermuda was a small island, and there were only so many cases he could work on before his cover was blown. The drug dealers would have killed him had he stayed on the force. He had never forgiven himself for leaving the force, and he felt that the drug crisis in Bermuda had only gotten worse since his departure.

His thoughts were interrupted when Bucko yelled out, "Captain! Look off the starboard. I see a vessel."

Turk quickly picked up his monocular and focused in on Bucko's location. He yelled back, "Roger that, mate." Sure enough it was a forty foot sail boat with the sails ripped and shredded. Turk yelled out, "All hands on deck! We've got a hot one."

Within minutes all hands were on deck. His crew was made up of five ship hands. First there was Bucko, a Portuguese sailor and First Mate of 'The Rusty Bucket". They were lifelong friends, and Turk could trust him with his life.

Next there was Mulate, a transplant from Jamaica, who looked white but was from a mixed marriage, and most of the time he preferred his dark side. He was an expert at navigating the waters of the Caribbean, but he was also good with the ship's electronic systems.

The third shipmate, Jawz, was dark skinned and one of the most qualified scuba divers in Bermuda. Over the last three years, he had been responsible for finding more submerged treasure than the rest of the crew altogether.

Then there was Squid who was white, and although small in stature, he was big in heart and could hold his own with anyone.

The last member of the crew was Mugger, a dark skinned and very large man. With his massive six foot six inch, three hundred fifty pound frame, Mugger could outwork any three men.

With the crew on deck, everyone was focused on the sailboat that appeared to be adrift. As they drew near Turk barked out, "Squid, you and Mulate check out below deck and look for survivors. Mulate, while you're down there check out their radio gear and any last transmissions."

Mulate yelled back, "Got it, mon." Squid nodded his head in agreement.

Turk turned to the others and said, "The rest of us will tie her up on our starboard side."

As they pulled alongside the sailboat Mugger and Jawz jumped aboard. They quickly secured her to the tug. From the bridge Bucko yelled down, "This forty foot yawl is a real beauty. It should be worth a tidy sum, Captain."

Turk yelled back as he jumped aboard the sailboat, "You got that bloody well right, mate." The ship was deserted. There was no trace of anyone on the deck dead or alive.

Mulate and Squid went below deck. After a few minutes of scrounging around Mulate reappeared. He threw three packages up on the deck as he emerged and yelled out, "Look mon, cocaine bricks. The whole forward cabin is filled with them. We'll be millionaires!" Everyone else just stood there mesmerized by the bricks of cocaine, except Turk.

Turk walked up and kicked one of the bricks across the deck and yelled out, "That's bloody bull shit, mate! I want every brick cut opened and dumped overboard. We'll take the empty wrappings back to Bermuda for the authorities."

Mulate snapped back, "Come on mon, give this Jamaican a break. I was only kidding."

Turk was still pissed off. When it came to illegal drugs he didn't kid around. He hated drug smugglers with a passion. Turk added, "Bring that crap top side, cut the bricks open and dump them overboard. We'll turn the empty bags over to the authorities when we dock in Bermuda."

Squid asked, "Are you sure we can do that without getting into trouble?"

Turk gave Squid a look that could kill and said, "Damn it! You heard what I said. Let's get busy." Without saying another word the entire crew started a line of passing the cocaine bricks from the forward cabin to the upper deck. Up on the deck Mugger slit the bricks open while Jawz dumped the cocaine overboard. This process took over three hours to complete. By the time they were done it was dusk. Squid went back aboard the tug to fix dinner while the others secured the sailboat and prepared it to be towed back to Bermuda.

That night in the galley everyone sat around talking about the new found sailboat except Mulate, who had drawn the short straw to stay aboard the sailboat for the night to make sure it stayed secured to the tug. While drinking a beer Jawz said, "I bet that sailboat must be worth two hundred thousand dollars in Bermuda. Why in the hell would these drug smugglers abandon this sailboat and a small fortune in drugs?"

Squid replied, "Well, mate, don't forget we just happen to be in the Bermuda Triangle."

Jawz spoke up, "So are you suggesting that the Triangle swallowed them up?"

Turk added, "Hell no, what he's saying is that the bloody idiots were washed overboard in that storm we had a few days ago."

Bucko snapped back, "No matter what, they were bloody drug smugglers and I could care less what happened to them."

Turk picked up his bottle of beer and said, "Cheers, mates, to our good fortune and the drug smugglers' bad fortune." With that everyone clicked their bottles. After that Turk added, "That's it for me, mates. It's sack time. We've got a long day tomorrow getting back to Bermuda. Maybe by tomorrow night we'll pull into St. George's Harbour and have a cold one at the Shinbone Pub."

4

CHAPTER 2

Harbor Patrol

HARBOR PATROL

About ten pm the next night the tug and its tow were about a mile out of St. George's Harbour. Bucko had already reported to Harbour Radio announcing The Rusty Bucket's arrival plus that they were towing a sailboat. By the time they were in the narrow channel entering the harbour all hands were on deck. Mugger and Jawz were on the sailboat with Turk, Bucko, Squid and Mulate on the tug. Bucko and Turk were in the bridge with Bucko working the ship's wheel. Turk was keeping his eyes out on the harbour watching for unexpected boats. As they grew closer to King's Square, Turk spotted two Harbour Police Patrol boats on a dead-head course coming for them at a high rate of speed with their sirens blaring.

Turk slammed his fist down on the rail and yelled out, "What the bloody hell do the cops want with us?"

Bucko replied, "Not sure Captain, but we're going to find out in a moment.

Turk in an annoyed voice said, "Stop engines. Wait here while I go down and see what the hell they want." When Turk made his way to the aft side of the tug Squid and Mulate were already there waiting for them. They all just stood there and waited for the patrol boats to pull alongside.

As the boats drew near to each other a voice through a megaphone yelled out, "Stop your engines and lay down your weapons, or we'll blast your bloody butts out of the water."

Turk couldn't believe what he was hearing. These cops must think they were drug smugglers. Then it dawned on him who the voice on the megaphone was. Turk yelled back, "Savage, you son of a bitch, it's me Turk Black."

The voice yelled back, "I know who it is and my sources say you're smuggling drugs now, Turk."

Turk yelled back, "That's bull shit, Savage, and you know it."

As the two patrol boats tied up to both sides of the tug, Inspector Savage stepped aboard and said, "Well, Turk, we'll just see about that." He turned to two of his officers and said, "Go check out that sailboat first and then we'll search the tug. Savage looked back at Turk and said, "You and your mates have a seat and stay out of our way.'

Turk started to say something, but before he could Savage yelled, "Oh did I also say, keep your bloody mouths shut before we shut them." Turk sat down on the tugs deck in disgust and waited.

After waiting twenty minutes the two officers climbed back on the tug from the sailboat with their arms full of empty white powdery plastic bags. Turk spoke first saying, "Look I told you mate we did nothing wrong. We found cocaine on this abandon sailboat and we dumped it over board."

The second officer stepped forward and said, "Inspector, look at this."

Savage took the objects from him and turned back around facing Turk saying, "And what the bloody hell is this, a brick of flour?"

Turk couldn't believe his eyes. He looked around at all his shipmates for an answer, but they were all speechless. Turk had double checked just to make sure they had disposed of all of the cocaine. Now Turk just shook his head in disgust. He didn't need to say anything; he knew the drill.

Savage took over pointing at both of the boats saying, "You officers cuff his crew and take them back to the station. And tow these boats behind you." As he cuffed Turk he said, "You're coming with me, mate. We've got something special planned for you."

Turk snapped back, "Oh yeah, what is it? Are you going to try to force a confession out of me?"

Savage laughed and said, "We don't have to; your goose is already cooked." The two sat in the boat quietly for the rest of the boat ride back to the dock. Once there Savage shoved Turk into a police car with its lights flashing. They quickly passed the St. George's police station. Turk looked over to Savage and said, "Where're you taking me--- Westgate's or the Hamilton Police station?"

Savage smiled and said, "Well, old buddy, you'll just have to wait."

While they drove along Turk just couldn't understand how Savage could be doing this to him. Over the years, they had worked cases together, and he thought they were friends. The speeding patrol car had by-passed Hamilton and was still on North Shore road so there was no way they were going to Westgate's Prison either. They turned onto St. John's Place Road and turned into the Governors House Estate. The car pulled around to the back side of the massive mansion. Before he knew what was happening he was whisked out of the car and through a door that led below ground. Turk turned to Savage and said as they walked down the narrow corridor, "So the torture chamber is down here?"

Savage just pushed on Turk's shoulder and said, "Just keep moving; you'll see soon enough. At the end of the hallway the pair walked up to a wide steel door where two officers were standing by each side of the door. As they drew near, one guard reached over and pulled the door open allow-ing the pair to enter the room. The room was dark and before they knew it the door slammed behind them. Turk thought to himself, "Oh crap! Someone down here is going to blow a hole through my head, and that will be the end of me."

CHAPTER 3

Enemy of The State

ENEMY OF THE STATE

Still in the dark, Turk was abruptly placed in a chair with Savage standing behind him. A few moments later a door in front of them opened, and the lights were turned on. Turk struggled to focus on the person who had just walked into the room and then had sat behind a massive desk. As Turk's sight returned he was shocked to see he was in the presence of the Governor of Bermuda, Nathaniel Butler.

The Governor was first to speak, "Well, Mr. Black, I'm sorry for the mysterious circumstances, but it's nice to finally meet you."

Turk stood up to shake his hand, but realized his hands were still cuffed. The Governor saw his predicament and said, "Inspector, don't you think it's about time to un-cuff our guest?"

Savage nodded and said, "Yes sir." He then pulled out a key from his pocket and removed the cuffs from Turk.

After rubbing his wrists Turk turned to the Governor asking, "Your honor, what the hell am I doing here if you don't mind me asking?"

The Governor smiled and replied, "Well Mr. Black, you've been caught bringing cocaine into Bermuda with the intent to sell."

Turk replied, "That's not true, your honor."

The Governor added, "Well, that's what it looks like and that what's tomorrow morning's newspaper is going to read."

Savage walked over to Turk and said, "Sit down, mate. You've got options here. Listen to the Governor." Turk sat down in quietly and with his hand gestured for the Governor to continue.

The Governor went on to say, "Our country is at war. We're being attacked from all sides, and we're losing. What is this war we're losing? It's the war on drugs. The drug lords and drug dealers are using our laws against us, and frankly they have us out gunned. Young man, I'm about to take you to a fork in the road, and your future will depend on which fork you take."

Turk was a bit confused, but very interested. He said, "Go on, sir."

The Governor continued, "Three to four hundred years ago when these colonial islands' future was at stake, the local Governors gave buccaneers and privateers a Letter of Marque. This was a license to kill, I suppose. This commission granted by the Governor authorizes its recipient to search, seize and destroy assets belonging to enemies of the state. This also affords one protection under the Governor. In fact one of my ancestors who I am named after was also a Governor of Bermuda and a commissioned privateer for the Crown himself."

Turk then asked, "So why am I getting a history lesson, sir?"

Savage thumped Turk on the back of his head with his hand and said, "Stupid, he's also talking about you. You're going to become a modern day buccaneer, mate."

Turk asked, "Are you telling me that I can just go out on the streets and bust any suspected drug dealer and shoot them down?"

The Governor added, "Not in the streets, but yes on the open seas. Your Letter of Marque specifically states the waters of the Bermuda Triangle. Is that clear? We're going to war and will attack our enemies before they reach the shores of Bermuda."

Turk nodded his head and said, "So the government of Bermuda is giving me a Letter of Marque. Is that right?"

The Governor smiled and said, "Not exactly. Back in 1856 the British government signed the Treaty of Paris which abolished privateering."

Getting angry Turk yelled, "So is there a bloody letter or not?"

The Governor replied, "Calm down."

Before he could finish, another figure stepped out of the shadows and said, "Yes, there is a letter, and it's signed by the Speaker of the House of the United States House of Representatives. The US government never signed the treaty of 1856. In fact Article I, Section 8, paragraph 11 of the U.S. Constitution authorizes Congress to grant Letters of Marque and Reprisal."

Savage went over and gave the man who had just spoken a hug. He then said, "You bloody bastard, it's good to see you, mate." It was Special FBI Agent Derrick Storm. Savage knew him well. The two friends had been to hell and back on past assignments. Savage would give his life for Storm, and Storm felt the same way about Savage. Savage turned back to Turk saying, "I trust this man with my life and so should you. You can take what he says to the bloody bank."

Turk, trying to lower his blood pressure, stood up and said, "Alright, so how does the United States fit into this?"

Storm replied, "That will become much clearer later. Be patient and be assured that the United States government also wants the drug trafficking eradicated." Turk asked again, "Ok, but what about bringing these criminals to justice? Will the actions and seizures we make on the open seas be admissible in court?"

Savage stepped back into the conversation saying, "Look mate, if you get into a bloody sea skirmish with these smugglers and blow them out of the water, then nobody's going to court. You're just going to have some missing drug dealers and drug couriers. If you capture these goons, simply tie them up, disable their engines, put out a distress call to the local authorities no matter what the country. Then get the hell out of there. You'll be nothing, but a phantom."

Turk added, "I like that. We'll be phantom marauders. I suppose you already know that the South American drug lords will have a bounty of millions on our heads?"

The Governor replied, "This is where Bermuda enters the picture. We cannot give you a Letter of Marque, but we can provide you with safe haven. That's why you'll only be safe in your home port of Bermuda, providing you arrive in the dark of night."

Turk asked, "Why's that?"

Savage added, "Don't forget that after tonight you're out on bail awaiting trial for drug possession with the intent to distribute."

Turk snapped back, "What the hell do you mean— awaiting trial?"

Savage replied, "Alright, alright. We're giving you a cover. The local drug dealers will hear about your arrest, and you'll become one of them. No one will even think about you when the word gets out about someone taking out drug boats."

Turk added, "I guess I'll just be a scum bucket that goes with The Rusty Bucket."

Savage added, "Speaking of The Rusty Bucket, you won't be cruising around in that tug anymore. As of tonight it's impounded."

Turk looked at the Governor and said, "Is Savage crazy? You want me to stop the flow of drugs on the open seas, and now you take away my boat?"

The Governor smiled and said, "Now look, Turk. We never said you were going out to sea in that old tug. Believe me, we have a ship for you that any captain in the world would die for."

Turk nodded his head. The Governor went on to say, "Look, let's be honest. Sooner or later you're going to have the authorities from other countries trying to track you down and if you're not careful maybe even Bermuda.

You have to stay a shadow in the mystique of the Bermuda Triangle to survive. I'm giving your letter to Inspector Savage to keep for you. This may be your only ticket home some day." The Governor hesitated for a few seconds and then said, "Enough of this, you and Savage have another stop to make before the night is over." He shook Turk's hand and said, "Good luck, Turk. Tonight we've declared war on the drug world. There's no turning back."

Storm patted both men on the back and said, "Just remember, Turk. We'll be tracking your whereabouts and if you ever need me, I'll be there and we'll have your backside." He turned to Savage saying, "Get your butt out of my sight before you drag me into some more trouble."

Turk turned to Savage and said, "So much for this reunion. Come on mate, let's go kick some butt."

As Savage and Turk left the room Savage laughed, "What the bloody hell do you mean, let's?"

CHAPTER 4

The Phantom

THE PHANTOM

Savage and Turk were dropped off by a patrol car at Albouys Point in Hamilton where a Bermuda Police patrol boat was waiting for them. As they stepped on board, Turk looked around and said, "Where the bloody hell is my crew? I've got news for you, Savage, I'm not going anywhere without my mates."

Savage laughed and said, "Your bloody mates are waiting for you on their new ship. That is if they haven't already left your worthless butt behind."

Turk plopped himself down in a seat and said, "That's damn funny, Savage."

The patrol boat slowly pulled away from Albouys Point and out into the darkness of the Great Sound. Turk looked over at Savage and asked, "Where the hell are we going?"

Savage replied, "We're going to the one place on the island that you've never been to, and frankly you don't even know it exists."

Turk replied, "Don't bullshit me, Savage. Bermuda is a small island. They're no secrets here."

Savage smilingly said, "We'll see, we'll see." He turned back around and stared out over the bow of the boat ignoring Turk for the rest of the trip.

After about fifteen minutes cruising across the Great Sound, Turk could see they were closing in on Morgan's Point. For over fifty years Morgan's

Point had been a United States Naval Air Station Annex. He thought to himself that there was no way a large boat could be docked there without being seen. But what Turk hadn't thought about was that Morgan's Island had never been opened to the public since the United States Navy had pulled out of Bermuda. The small abandoned peninsula had been sealed off by the Bermuda Government because it had been reported that the United States Navy had used the island as a dump site for toxic pollutants and fill.

The long narrow inlet to this peninsula was heavily wooded on both sides and faced west away from the Great Sound making it unable to be seen from the water. This small harbour was the perfect hiding place for a small ship, especially a stealth ship that couldn't be spotted from the air.

As the boat cruised over six hundred feet into the small harbour Turk could see off the starboard side of the boat a massive concrete retaining wall on the shoreline. The wall began to split apart in the middle and parted into two sections creating a massive opening that the patrol boat could pass through. Just after they passed between the massive concrete walls they closed behind them. In the total blackness of the moment Turk yelled out, "So Savage, this is how you're going to get rid of me. Leave me in a black hole."

Turk couldn't see Savage, but he could hear him. Savage belted out, "You impatient bastard, give it a minute!" A few seconds later the lights in the half submerged alcove came on. Turk rubbed his eye not believing what he was looking at.

Savage smiled as he watched Turk stare. Savage went on to say, "This is the latest and greatest top secret British super stealth ship ever built. The super ship had been built to help fight the war on terror and to be used by the Royal Marines. This slender and sleek fifty foot super ship is a light blue gray color designed to be invisible from detection from the air. Its stealth design and built-in technology will keep any radar system from detecting its presence. This ship has the capability of out running or catching any other boat or ship in the world. This super ship can reach speeds of over seventy five miles per hour in seconds. The ships engines are a hybrid of diesel and electric turbine motors. Under the right conditions an enemy will not see or hear this boat coming."

Savage turned to Turk and said, "Well, Captain Turk, would you like a tour of your new ship?"

Turk smiled and replied, "Yes sir!" The two men climbed aboard the boat and walked towards the bow. While they were walking Turk stopped and asked, "Where in the hell are the ship's weapons? Sooner or later we're going to have to stand and fight."

Savage was waiting for this question. He smiled and snapped his finger and yelled, "Weapons Officer! Show us your fire power."

A voice from the bridge yelled back, "Aye sir." He went on to say, "Torpedoes." Just then on the starboard and aft side of the boat three sets of torpedo tubes rolled out of the boats rails on each side of the ship. The weapons officer next yelled out, "Gatling gun." A large Gatling gun quickly rose from below the aft deck of the boat. The voice then yelled out, "depth charges." A steel box at the bow of the boat lid slid back revealing two rows of gallon sized canisters of depth charges. The voice from the bridge yelled out, "All weapons." Over the next two minutes weapons popped up all over the boat from small anti-aircraft guns to flame throwers to grenade launchers and miniature rocket launchers.

Turk stood back in disbelief saying, "Holy Crap! This bloody ship could take on the Royal Navy. We are definitely going to put a dent in the drug world."

Savage snapped back, "We're not looking for a dent, Turk. We're looking for total destruction and devastation of drug trafficking in Her Majesties Territories and the waters around the United States." Savage went on to say, "I don't want to rain on your parade, but don't forget none of the countries in the waters you'll be patrolling will even know of your exist-ence. In fact they may consider you an enemy target. By the way, mate, what are you going to christen this little ship?"

Turk thought for a minute and said, "Well, mate, since our home for the foreseeable future is in the Bermuda Triangle I think this sleek lady should be christened 'The Phantom'. The drug world is about to become a believer in the Bermuda Triangle. The Phantom of the Night will kick their asses."

Savage smiled and added, "Let's hope you're right. Now, would you like to meet your new crew?"

Turk's face turned red. He grabbed Savage by the collar and yelled, "What the hell do you mean— new crew? What the hell happened to my old crew?"

Savage looked at Turk and said, "You better remove your hands from my collar before I snap them in half." Turk let go of his collar and stepped back. Savage said, "Thank you, mate." He went on to say, "You hot head, you still have your old crew, but you've also got some new crew members."

Turk snapped back, "What the hell do I need more crew members for? The ones I have now are perfect."

Savage starred at Turk and said, "Listen, mate, you're going to need more help to run this ship."

Turk asked, "My crew has been with me for years. How can I trust these unknowns?"

Savage continued on, ""Look mate, my best friend, Special Agent of the FBI Derrick Storm has handpicked this crew. In fact, Derrick Storm is the only agent in the entire United States government that has knowledge of our secret operation." Savage looked up at the bridge and yelled out, "Alright, mates, let's have the entire crew down on the deck for inspection."

One by one Turk's crew members slid down the bridge rail onto the deck. First there was Bucko followed by Mulate with Jawz not far behind him. Next there was Squid and Mugger. A minute later the three new crew members walked onto the deck and stood at the end of the line.

Savage and Turk walked over to the new crew members. Savage spoke up first saying, "Turk, this is Gunner. He's your new weapons specialists. He's an expert with all the ship's weapons and will help train the others." Turk shook his hand and stepped over to the next new crew member. Savage added, "This is Dawg. He's an ex- Navy Seal and your best hand-to-hand fighter on board. Nothing will stop him in a dog fight. He'll keep coming at you." Next they stepped over to the last new crew member. "This is Saber." Turk couldn't help noticing her long silky black hair. She was African American with the most intoxicating aquamarine eyes he had ever seen. Savage elbowed Turk to keep him from staring and continued to say, "She's an expert diver and a trained medic, plus she can probably kick your ass."

Turk replied, "Right!"

Savage stepped back with his arm around Turk and said, "Well, mate, this is it. You have your commission from the Governor and the protection of the Crown and the United States Government to free the waters of the Bermuda Triangle of all enemies of the Crown and the United States Government. You and your crew will have twenty four hours to make your ship seaworthy for the open seas and leave the protection of Bermuda. Remember, when you enter or depart the protected waters of Bermuda it must be under the cover of darkness. The Phantom can never be associated with Bermuda or the Governor will order its destruction with whatever means he has at his disposal. Is that clear, Turk?"

Turk smiled and said, "This ship has more firepower than the entire Bermuda police force and the Bermuda Regiment. How can he bloody do that?"

Savage snapped back, "Don't get cocky! The British Government and the United States Government would back the Governor in hours." Savage shook Turk's hand and went on to say, "May the powers of the Bermuda Triangle be with you all." Savage turned away from Turk and walked over to the patrol boat. As the boat pulled away Savage shouted, "Oh, by the way, Turk, the cocaine bricks we found on your old tug were accidently planted there by one of my officers." Before Turk could respond the boat shot out of the alcove like a bat out of hell. Turk finally yelled out, "Savage! Next time I see you, you're bloody butt will be on the line." He knew Savage never heard him, but he still felt better.

Although still very pissed at what he just heard Savage say, Turk turned to his crew and yelled out, "You all heard Savage. Let's get this red hot mama ready for battle and go kick some drug smugglers asses. Dismissed!"

CHAPTER 5

Let the Hunt Begin

LET THE HUNT BEGIN

As Turk made his first inspection of the Phantom he was amazed at the discipline of the crew including his old crew. He could tell that before his arrival aboard, his old crew must have had a briefing on the operations of the ship. Every member of the crew seemed to know exactly what was expected of them and what to do. The concealed alcove was not only a dock for the ship it was also a warehouse that must have had over ten thousand square feet of warehouse space. There was everything from food supplies to weapons storage for every armament on the ship. Turk walked over to the gunwhale where Gunner was standing and asked, "Who in the hell keeps track of this inventory?"

Gunner replied, "That's simple. When we leave a team will come in and replace anything we've used. So when we return to port next we can restock our ship."

Turk smiled and added, "Sounds like a plan to me." He thought for a minute and asked, "Do we have any other ports in the Caribbean?"

Gunner smiled back at Turk and said, "Not a one, sir. Once we leave this port we're on our own."

Turk replied, "I see." He then yelled out to the rest of the crew, "Don't skimp on the ammo, the rum, the beer, the cigars and the popcorn." Turk walked off continuing with his inspection.

Saber had heard Turk's command. She turned to Dawg and said, "What's our new Captain think this is, a party barge?"

Dawg laughed and said, "Yeah baby, I think I'm going to like this dude."

Saber snapped back, "Don't call me baby, you baboon, and the Captain's name is Turk, not dude." She turned and walked back into the warehouse.

Dawg yelled out, "Get me some beer too while you're at it."

Saber yelled back not losing her stride, "Sure thing, Deputy Dog, but first I'm getting myself a couple of bottles of wine and some cheese."

Dawg smiled and went back to work.

Turk finally made his way to the bridge. He walked over to the intercom system. He picked up the mike with his hand and clicked the button on the side of the mike allowing him to speak over the intercom system. Turk spoke through the mike saying, "Testing 1254". He lowered the mike from his mouth for a few seconds then raised it back to his mouth again. He now clicked the mike and said, "All hands at seventeen hundred hour meet on the bridge, over and out mates." After ten seconds Turk came back on the intercom saying, "Bring your own drinks or whatever floats your boat."

Gunner and Bucko were in their cabin working on their bunks when they heard Turk's announcement. Gunner looked puzzled. He asked Bucko, "What the hell is he telling us?

Bucko replied, "The Captain's telling us drink up mates, cause when we set sail all booze is locked down until further notice."

Gunner added, "Crap! Now I feel like I'm back in the US Navy."

Bucko laughed and said, "Get used to it, mate."

At seventeen hundred hours all hands were on deck. Turk looked over the crew. He was very impressed with his crew, but he would probably never tell them that. After pacing for awhile Turk stopped and said, "I'm not a man of many words, but tonight you might get a few. After dark tonight The Phantom goes out on her maiden voyage. All I can tell you is we're heading south deep into the Bermuda Triangle."

Saber spoke up and asked, "Captain, is that a bad thing?"

Turk replied, "As far as I'm concerned the Bermuda Triangle is a defined area of the Atlantic Ocean where storms can get out of control, but nothing else beyond that. Now if you don't mind I'd like to continue." No one else had any other questions. Turk went on to say, "You all know what our mission is. Yes, we're privateers with the Governor's commission to declare war on the drug lords who enter the Bermuda Triangle. We ask no questions; we seize drugs. We may or may not have to kill these smugglers. If they resist, they will surely die. If they surrender, they will be cast afloat in hopes that the local authorities will find them. We follow no legal protocol and are not bound by the laws of any country. In fact, we might find ourselves under attack by authorities from other countries. This alcove is our only safe haven providing we enter it in the still of the night. If we're seen we might be arrested. Now that I've detailed what our mission is, if there are any of you who don't agree you are free to leave. Everyone else will sail thirty minutes after dark." Turk left the crew and went below without saying another word.

The crew all looked at each other for a few minutes. Finally Bucko said, "Daylight's burning. This ship is setting sail in less than an hour. We better get off our dead asses and get this boat ship shape. The rest of the crew took Bucko's lead and began the final preparations.

CHAPTER 6

The King of Cocaine

THE KING OF COCAINE

In a hidden harbour not far from Guantánamo Bay in Cuba is the home of "The King of Cocaine" of the Caribbean, Zorra MÁXIMO. From this one location more cocaine is distributed throughout the Caribbean, South Florida and Bermuda than the entire country of Colombia exports. Nobody knows if this secret drug smuggling operation is known, condoned, or financed by the Cuba government. Some believe that after the fall of the Communist government of Soviet Union and their subsequent pullout from Cuba, the Cuban government was desperate for funding to prevent the island's economic collapse.

Zorra MÁXIMO has always been well connected with the Cuban Revolution. In fact, in his younger years he was a captain in the Cuban army and has had many tours of duty leading guerilla forces in Africa and South America. MÁXIMO is a large man. His six foot two inch three hundred pound frame makes him stand out whenever he enters a room. He is constantly surrounded by body guards of equal stature.

With state-of-the-art surveillance and tracking equipment, the United States base at Guantánamo is constantly tracking his movement, but to no avail. As long as MÁXIMO stays clear of Guantánamo Bay the United States is helpless to stop him. He is constantly taunting the base with fake shipments in hope of provoking an international incident between Cuba and the United States.

MÁXIMO has a fleet of high speed Chris Craft Stinger boats he has purchased over the years on the black market. With this fleet of drug smuggling boats the authorities from any of the surrounding countries have little chance of apprehending his drug shipments.

MÁXIMO has four lieutenants to carry out his bidding. They have all been with him for years and they would take a bullet for their drug lord. Bruno, Armando and Benito were cut out of the same mold. They are ruthless cold blooded killers who kill first and don't ask questions later. Gitmo is the forth lieutenant who took his name from the US base. He's a serial killer who loves to torture his victims if he gets a chance.

Zorra MÁXIMO and his lieutenants rule his empire with a bloody iron fist. He's at the top of the food chain in Cuba and throughout his dominion. There is absolutely no one to challenge him for his drug empire. The Colombian drug lords fear him and would stay out of his territory fearing reprisals of death and destruction.

With the start of a new week, MÁXIMO had traveled to his cocaine fortress and was awaiting his lieutenants to report last week's take and this week's activities. One by one his henchmen arrived and sat at the boardroom style table. MÁXIMO looked across the table at Benito and said, "Benito, my brother, tell me what good news you have for me this week."

Benito replied, "The take last week in Florida excluding Miami was two million dollars. I expect the same this week."

MÁXIMO replied, "Very good, my brother." He next looked at Armando and nodded his head.

Knowing it was his turn to report, Armando said, "My lord, the Caribbean is up over twenty five percent to one point seven million dollars. With no hurricanes in the forecast the outlook is good for this week."

MÁXIMO as he lit his cigar said, "Armando, you never let me down." His eyes passed over Bruno as if something was wrong and he went on to Gitmo and asked, "Gitmo, how is our family business doing in Miami?"

Gitmo replied, "MÁXIMO, I found a snitch who was going to tell the cops about a couple of our drop zones. Now he talks no more as he is missing his tongue."

MÁXIMO added, "Very good, Gitmo. That should be a reminder for others not to talk to cops. Please continue."

Gitmo continued, "Our take in Miami last week was one million dollars. We should do better this week."

MÁXIMO turned back to Bruno and said, "Bruno, what do you have to report on Bermuda?"

Bruno hesitated for a minute, but before he could say anything MÁXIMO yelled out, "Don't even try to candy coat your report, Bruno!"

Bruno knew he was in trouble. He took a big gulp and said, "My lord, last week we lost our shipment bound for Bermuda in the Bermuda Triangle."

MÁXIMO turned blood red and screamed as he pounded on the table, "Don't bullshit me, Bruno! There's no such thing as the Bermuda Triangle. You've got five minutes to explain yourself before I slit your throat."

Bruno continued, "The boat was towed into St George's Harbour by a treasure hunter who's an ex-cop. My sources on the streets say he was arrested on the water before making port. He and his crew were thrown in jail, and his boat was impounded."

MÁXIMO yelled, "So where in the hell is my cocaine?"

A bit sheepishly, Bruno said, "We don't know if this guy dumped it somewhere or if the Bermuda police have it impounded."

MÁXIMO added, "Who in the hell is this ex-cop? And why don't you have some of our friends on the inside of the jail persuade him to talk?"

Bruno added, "More bad news, boss. His name is Turk Black, and because he's an ex-cop he made bail. They even took his crew off to some lock down place where we don't have any contacts."

MÁXIMO pounded the table again and yelled, "Bruno, this is your problem. You fix it and get my cocaine back or you're a dead man. Tomorrow you're personally going to take another boatload of cocaine to Bermuda. You'll sell it at a premium to help recover our losses, and you'll find my lost cocaine shipment or the million dollars it would have sold for. Get you're dead ass out of my sight. I don't want to see you again until you've made things right."

Without saying a word Bruno stood up from his chair and walked out of the room slamming the door behind him.

MÁXIMO threw a bottle of beer striking the other side of the door. The beer bottle exploded everywhere. MÁXIMO laughed and left the room without saying another word, leaving his remaining lieutenants in silence just sitting there staring at each other.

In a matter of hours Bruno had one of his two Stinger high speed boats loaded full of cocaine, weapons, and his thugs. He was going to find his cocaine or kill anyone who got in his way. He had no fear of the Bermuda authorities. Bruno knew that most of the time they didn't carry firearms. By the time they would be issued, it would be too late. Bruno would have already done his damage.

Bruno and his two Stingers shot out of their hidden harbour like rockets on their way to a target. As they blasted by the entrance to Guantánamo Bay they fired their automatic weapon towards the base to taunt them.

Soon they would be on the open seas on a direct course towards Bermuda going right through the Bermuda Triangle.

CHAPTER 7

Surprise on the High Seas

SURPRISE ON
THE HIGH SEAS

It was almost midnight in Bermuda. The Phantom was slowly cruising out of its hidden harbour at Morgan's Point. The ship was running on battery power so no one on land or in the Great Sound would detect her presence. Turk, Bucko, Gunner and Saber were all on the ship's bridge assisting on her maiden voyage out of Bermuda. As Turk stood on the bridge overlooking the Great Sound he was taken back by the total blackness of the night except for the lights that dotted the shoreline and the stars in the sky. They almost ran together. All of a sudden he was jarred back to reality by a nudge from Bucko. Turk turned to Bucko and asked, "What is it mate?"

Bucko replied, "Look off the port side. A harbour patrol boat is approaching us, Captain."

Turk turned to Gunner and yelled out, "Gunner, prepare to blow that patrol boat out of the water."

Gunner with a puzzled look on his face said, "What the hell did you just say?"

Turk laughed saying, "Just kidding, unless that bastard Inspector Savage is on that patrol boat." Turk went on to say, "Gunner, let's find out what this Phantom has to offer. Give me stealth mode and full generator power, and we'll see what our local harbour patrol boys are thinking." He turned to Saber and said, "Saber, turn to the police radio frequency and let's see what they have to say."

Saber replied, "Roger that, Captain."

Gunner set the stealth mode and kicked in the turbines. Within seconds the Phantom had hit forty knots and was accelerating. Turk had already taken over the ship's wheel and was on a direct line towards the patrol boat. At the last possible second Turk swerved the Phantom and ran along side of the patrol boat throwing a wake of water over the boat that almost drowned the officers. The Phantom left the patrol boat in its wake in seconds. As the Phantom was leaving the Sound they could hear a distress call from the patrol boat, "Base come back; this is patrol boat ten. We're in trouble."

The base operator on duty replied, "Boat ten, this is base. Report your situation."

The officer on boat ten replied, "Our engines are out. We were swamped by a massive rogue wave that hit us from nowhere."

The base operator replied, "Is everyone alright?"

The officer on the patrol boat added, "Yes, except for being soaked and a dead engine." He went on to say, "We need a tow."

The base operator replied, "Roger that. I've got your coordinates and another patrol boat is on its way."

Bucko flipped the ships speaker off and looking over at Turk said, "Those bloody coppers never knew what hit them."

Saber interrupted by saying, "You're lucky you goons didn't drown those poor police officers."

Turk, a bit annoyed said, "Alright missy, calm down. There was no harm done."

Saber turned her back to Turk and walked out of the bridge. Turk yelled to the others saying, "Alright the party's over. It's back to work. We need to be out of Bermuda waters before daybreak."

They had already left the island behind them. Bucko turned off the ships stealth mode and slowly shut down the electric turbines as he fired up the diesel engines. Turk and his crew didn't know it, but they were heading on a collision course towards Bruno and his pair of Stinger boats.

The next two days were very uneventful. Turk had the Phantom on a zig zag course as they headed south towards the Caribbean on a constant lookout for drug smugglers. Turk made sure the days were not wasted. The crew was dropping into the ocean buoys with signs on them every fifty to one hundred miles. The signs read:

✗Drug Smugglers Beware✗

Enter the Bermuda Triangle

and Die!

If the signs didn't send the drug smugglers running then Turk would send them to Davy Jones Locker.

It was now almost dusk. The entire crew, except for Bucko, were in the ship's mess having dinner. Bucko had pulled the first watch of the night on the bridge. Later one of the crew would bring him his dinner while he was on watch.

Meanwhile Bucko was about to dose off when bells, sirens and buzzers began sounding off all over the bridge. Bucko jumped up out of his chair and ran over to the satellite GPS screen. After a quick review of the screen, Bucko slammed his fist down on the red pad on the counter. His action set off the ships early warning systems sending a blaring ear-piercing sound throughout the ship. Bucko yelled out over the intercom, "Captain! Two unidentified fast moving ships are on a collision course with the Phantom."

Within seconds Turk burst onto the bridge yelling out, "Bucko, how much time do we have?"

Bucko replied, "No more than three minutes, sir."

Turk grabbed the mike from Bucko and yelled out, "All hands prepare for hostile contact. It looks like we have a couple of high speed drug smugglers in our sites in less than two and a half minutes."

Meanwhile on one of the Stingers, one of Bruno's men reached over and tapped Bruno on the shoulder saying, "Boss, I saw a fairly large blip on the radar screen then the next second it was gone. It was on a collision course with us."

Bruno leaned over and looked at the radar screen. After seeing a blank screen he said, "Don't worry, my brother. It must have been a whale that surfaced for air and then submerged again." Little did Bruno know he was just about a minute away from the Phantom.

Back on the Phantom the entire crew was at their battle stations. Turk quickly looked around the bridge and then spoke through the mike, "In less than a minute we'll pass between both Stingers. By the time they see us it will be too late. Only fire warning shots over their heads. I want to first make sure they're drug smugglers, and secondly give them a chance to surrender."

A few seconds later the Phantom was passing between the two boats throwing waves and bullets over their decks. Bruno and his crew were left scrambling not knowing what the hell just hit them. The next thing they heard was a megaphone voice saying, "This is your only warning to turn off your engines; throw your weapons overboard and surrender."

Bruno screamed out to his men, "Light up the sky with bullets and turn the ocean into blood." Both boats used their speed to take evasive action and speed off in opposite directions. The plan was simple. Each boat would circle around and attack the Phantom from opposite directions catching Turk in a crossfire. In seconds both boats were firing hundreds of rounds from machine guns at the Phantom. Turk yelled out, "Mates, we got our bloody answer." He turned to the starboard side of the ship and yelled out, "Gunner, fix that Gatling gun on your target and blow those drug smuggling bastards to hell!"

Gunner replied, "Aye captain." Gunner let loose a barrage of fire that ripped the Stinger to pieces in seconds. The Stinger exploded into a million pieces lighting up the night skies for miles.

Before Turk could turn his attention to the other Stinger the remaining smugglers had already shut down their engines and were throwing their weapons overboard. Turk yelled out, "Bucko, take the wheel. I want everyone else on deck with your M16's."

The remaining smugglers stood up in their Stinger with both hands held high. Turk yelled out, "Who's in charge?"

One of the smugglers yelled back, "No one, amigo. He's dead. He was on the other boat."

Turk turned to his crew and said, "Mugger, Squid, and Dawg board that boat and permanently disable her engines." Turk turned back to the crew of the remaining Stinger and said, "One wrong move out of any of you deadbeats and you'll be as dead as your mates in the other boat."

Mugger, Squid and Dawg went aboard the Stinger while the rest of the Phantom's crew kept their M16's trained on the Cubans. Mugger and Dawg worked over the engines while Squid hid a homing signal device on the Stinger. Ten minutes later the three were back aboard the phantom.

As the Phantom began to pull away Saber and Jawz threw the crew several jugs of water.

One of the Cubans yelled out, "Amigos, what are we to do for food?"

Turk yelled back, "Eat that bloody white power you have onboard and go to hell."

Turk knew based on their proximity to the east coast of the United States the US Coast Guard would track the homing device and have them picked up in less than a day.

As the Phantom continued on its southerly trek Turk went over the ships intercom system and said, "Job well done, mates. That's two drug smugglers down and only a thousand more to go. Get some rest tonight. Who knows what tomorrow will bring? "

CHAPTER 8

Feeling the Sting

FEELING THE STING

Over the next few weeks the marauders wrecked havoc across the sea lanes of the Bermuda Triangle. The Phantom had sunk or set adrift eighteen drug trafficking boats and ships. From speed boats to sail boats to yachts, Turk and his crew were merciless with their pursuit of the drug smugglers. The authorities of the United States and the Caribbean Islands had never seen so many smugglers captured in the open seas with engine problems.

The drug lords were starting to accuse each other of hijacking their drug shipments. Even sending armed escorts out with the smugglers did not help. Either the shipments made their way to their destination or they were never heard from again or captured by the authorities. Almost instantly after being attacked, the communications were lost with the ship. There was never a mayday signal sent out to anyone. The authorities were quick studies. They now knew that when they picked up on an international distress frequency homing signal that they were most likely going to find drug smugglers tied up and secured with their illegal cargo.

Meanwhile back in Cuba MÁXIMO and his lieutenants were having a heated discussion on the state of their drug business.

MÁXIMO screamed out as he pounded on the table, "What the hell is going on? Is one of my men a traitor and selling me out for cash?"

Armando was the first one to speak up, "MÁXIMO, Bruno has been missing for weeks. Could he be the traitor?"

Benito added, "He may have stolen a shipment, but he could never have known about the other shipments. I think my brother is dead. He was killed for his cocaine."

Gitmo asked, "Do you think some greedy Bermudians did him in?"

MÁXIMO growled and said, "We've lost millions of dollars over the last few weeks and someone is going to pay with their lives. The Columbian drug lords all assure me that they are having the same problems with shipments to the US and the Caribbean. In fact they are ready to make available to us a group of paramilitary bounty hunters to catch and kill these traitorous bastards."

Benito asked, "Can we trust the Columbians? They would kill us if they had a chance."

MÁXIMO replied, "Yes I know, but I too would kill them if I had the chance also. We have no choice but to embrace the Columbian's offer until we find out who's stealing from us." MÁXIMO looked at Armando and said, "You will join the bounty hunters with two of your best men and protect our interest and report back to me daily."

Armando yelled back, "But, MÁXIMO..."

Before Armando could finish MÁXIMO pulled out a pistol and pointed it at Armando's head and pulled the trigger back. He then said, "Armando, be careful what you say. The next words out of your mouth might be your last."

Armando turned red with anger and yelled, "I can't do that."

MÁXIMO replied, "Very well, amigo. The choice is yours." Without hesitation, MÁXIMO pulled the trigger and blew a golf ball sized hole through Armando's head. From the force of the close range firing Armando flipped backwards out of his chair and sprawled on the brick floor with blood flowing in all directions. MÁXIMO turned to Benito and asked, "Do you have any problems working with the Columbians?"

Benito replied almost before MÁXIMO had finished speaking, "No sir! I'll be ready with my men when they arrive."

MÁXIMO added, "Wise answer, amigo." He went on to say, "This meeting is over." He stood up, picked up his cigar and bottle of rum, and left the room.

Gitmo and Benito remained in their chairs looking at each other and Armando's lifeless body on the floor. Finally after what seemed to be an eternity, the two lieutenants got up from their chairs and left the room without saying a word to each other.

CHAPTER 9

The Secret Cargo

THE SECRET CARGO

It was almost dusk onboard the Phantom. It had been a quiet day with no sign of ships or boats in this area of the Triangle. The Phantom was on automatic pilot while Mulate was relaxing in the Captain's chair. Tonight he had the first watch duty, but in reality, there was not much to watch. The Phantom was automated so much that there almost wasn't any reason to have someone on the bridge.

Meanwhile below in the galley Turk and the rest of the crew were eating dinner. Turk looked over the table and said, "Mates, we've done a great job so far, but we're only scratching the surface." Some of the large shipments of drugs end up in Bermuda in containers loaded on container ships. Just how in the bloody hell are we going to tackle those ships?"

Jawz was first to reply, "We don't do a damn thing, Captain. US Customs should be inspecting those containers when they leave port and Bermuda Customs should be inspecting the containers when they arrive in Bermuda."

Turk replied, "Yeah I know, but we all know it's a hell of a way to smuggle drugs into Bermuda."

Saber asked, "Do we even have any authority to board a container ship on the high seas?"

Turk smiled and said, "If the ship is within the waters of the Bermuda Triangle we have the rights to board any craft if we feel there's drugs on board."

Dawg chimed in, "That sounds like one hell of a time taking over a defenseless ship. Are we then going to look through every container on board? You know there must be hundreds of them on every ship."

Turk smiled again and added, "Now, that's a hell of a good question, and I'll bet old Gunner's got the answer."

Gunner reached down under the mess table pulling out two objects, one in each hand. He stood up and pointed at the crew what appeared to be pistols with megaphone barrels on them. When he pulled the trigger the solid clear front that looked like a nose cone of a rocket turned green. Gunner finally spoke up, "These babies are state-of-art miniature scanners designed to scan through steel, concrete and just about anything else to find illegal drugs. When they lock onto contra band the face goes from green to red. They have a range of fifty feet so you can scan up to five containers sitting side to side at once just by walking past them."

Turk looked at the others and said, "Now what do you mugs think?"

Squid asked, "What's the accuracy of these little drug busters?"

Gunner replied, "In the test, they had a success rate of over eighty-nine percent."

Saber added, "That's nice, Gunner, but how about in the real world?"

Turk spoke up first saying, "Gunner, I'll answer that. Mates, we're the guinea pigs on this operation."

Saber continued by saying, "So we somehow take over a friendly unsuspecting container ship on the high seas and inspect their cargo?"

Turk replied, "That's just about the size of it, mates."

Squid added, "You all know that once we overtake a container ship a distress call will go out before we board her. In fact, we'll be declared pirates on the high seas. The US Coast Guard will treat us like Somali pirates. They'll be on us like flies on honey."

Turk a little defensive said, "Why in the hell do you think we have a Letter of Marque from the United States Congress?"

Dawg asked, "So if we're captured all you do is pull out that letter of whatever?"

Turk replied, "Well, not exactly. Inspector Savage back in Bermuda has it in safe keeping for us."

Saber added, "Oh, what a relief! If they shoot first and ask questions later, we'll all be dead."

Turk snapped back, "Enough of this bloody doom and gloom talk. We have a job to do. In fact, let's break up this party because at dawn tomorrow we're going to intercept that container ship out of Jacksonville." Turk stood up and added, "Good night, mates. We've got a big day tomorrow." He walked out of the galley leaving the others staring at Gunner and the scanners.

Finally Dawg said, "Sounds like a date to me." He also left the galley. The rest were quick to follow.

Before daybreak the next morning Turk, Gunner, and Bucko were in the bridge standing around the map table plotting the course towards the container ship. They were also discussing the best way to board the ship. Turk went on to say, "We'll be in stealth mode and we'll come up to her bow side so we'll be undetected." He looked over at Gunner and asked, "Well, my man, what do you have to do to get our sorry butts on board without being noticed?"

Gunner replied, "Captain, there aren't too many options. This ship was never intended to take on a cargo ship."

Turk prodded him on, "So what the bloody hell is our option, mate?"

Gunner continued on, "We'll blast grappling hooks tied to ropes to their deck and snag the top rail. The ropes are knotted every eighteen inches which will help us climb up the ropes quickly."

Turk had a perplexed look on his face. He then said, "That's the best you got? That means all our big men will be left behind. They'll never be able to climb up a fifty foot rope. I'm not even sure I can do that. Our boarding party will be Saber, Squid, Dawg, Mulate and myself. It's not exactly our most fierce boarding party, but it will do."

Bucko added, "I wish I could be there to see Squid tell their crew not to resist, or he'll beat the crap out of them."

Turk replied, "That's enough, smartass." He turned to Gunner and said, "Go round up the crew and give them their assignments. We'll intercept the ship in a couple of hours."

As Turk had predicted, the Phantom had pulled alongside of the container ship undetected. While the boarding crew gathered Gunner pulled out his grappling gun and in rapid succession fired two grappling hooks that entangled themselves on the upper rails of the container ship. Gunner turned to the boarding crew holding out the ropes and said, "Well, who's bloody first? And who gets the "Drug Buster"?"

Turk spoke up first saying, "Well mate, that would be me." But before taking a rope he turned to the crew and pulled small shoulder pistols off his back. He flipped one to each of the boarding crew except for Saber. She got the Drug Buster.

Squid looked at his pistol in disgust and said, "Captain, all these guns are going to do is get us killed."

Turk laughed and added, "Look mate, we're not invading a hostile ship. We're just going to politely identify the cargo of drugs they have onboard. Now let's get going." Turk took the first rope and began pulling himself up the rope one hand after another. In a few minutes he had reached the top rail of the ship and climbed onboard unnoticed.

One after another Saber, Squid, Dawg and Mulate painfully climbed up the rope. Squid had the toughest time, but Dawg reached down from the top rail and helped pull Squid up. Turk turned to the group and said, "Team, follow me. We have to find the Captain first. After that we can split up." The small group was quick to make their way to the bridge. Once there, Turk preferred a dramatic entry so he kicked the bridge door open brandishing his paint gun in the air. The stunned Captain and his bridge crew gave up without a fight. Their hands went straight up in the air. Turk smiled and said, "Captain, you and your mates have nothing to worry about."

The Captain snapped back at Turk saying, "And who in the hell do you think you terrorists are?"

Turk still smiling replied, "First of all sir, we're not terrorists or even pirates. We're vigilante marauders. We are dedicated to keep the flow of illegal drugs and contra ban out of the waters of the Bermuda Triangle."

The Captain laughed and said, "How noble, but you're probably still thieves in the night looking for a quick score."

Turk cut the Captain off by saying, "Look mate, you can either embrace what we're about to show you or suffer the fallout. What will it be, Captain?"

The Captain reached down pulling open a drawer. In a second he was wheeling a small pistol, but before he could take aim at Turk, Turk in rapid fire ripped off three shots all striking the Captain in the chest. Red blood flew all over the bridge covering most of the ship's deckhands.

As the stunned Captain rolled around on the bridge floor Turk yelled out, "Get your ass up off the deck. You're not hurt. I only shot you with red paint balls.

The embarrassed Captain stood up, dripping with wet paint and said, "Alright, alright, whoever you are what we can do for you?"

Turk replied, "You escort my team and let us quickly scan your container cargo for drugs."

The Captain added, "Are you kidding? That will take a week to open each container on this ship."

Turk smiled and said, "Don't get nervous, Captain. We're only going to electronically scan your containers and mark the ones containing drugs so when you reach port in Bermuda the authorities can seize the property." Turk turned back to the Captain and said, "Follow me, I'll show you how the device works."

The small group went below deck to where the first row of containers had been stacked and secured. Turk turned to Saber and said, "Baby, do your thing."

Saber gave Turk a look that could kill for what he said. She then proceeded on to the first container. Saber pointed the scanner at the container as she passed by it, but there was no reaction to the scanner. Saber yelled out, "All clear" and went to the next container. Within seconds the scanners laser white beam began flashing green to red with a steady humming sound. Saber turned to Turk and said, "Bust it open, boss."

The ship's Captain laughed and said, "You're kidding." Turk and his crew did not respond to the Captain. They went about their work breaking open the container seal and opening the doors.

Meanwhile from a dark corner in the ships hold a mysterious character was quietly watching the events unfold. In one hand he was holding a pistol while in the other hand he was gripping a GPS phone.

Turk and Dawg cut the security straps and flipped up the dual levers releasing the locks holding the container doors closed. Once both doors were opened Turk turned to Saber and said, "Climb up in there and see if you can isolate whatever your scanner locked on."

Saber replied, "Thanks a lot." Just a few feet into the container she received a strong signal from the scanner. Saber yelled down to Turk," Pull this carton down, I think you'll find your contra ban in it."

Turk and Dawg reached up grabbing the carton and pulled it out onto the hold floor. Saber was quick to vacate the steaming hot container. Turk turned to the Captain and asked, "With your permission, Captain, I would like to instruct my men to open up the crate."

The Captain frowned, but still nodded his head with approval saying, "Permission granted."

Turk snapped his fingers. Dawg and Squid pulled out their boning knives and began slicing open the staves on the top of the wooden crate. Within seconds the lid was removed from the crate. Turk added, "Captain, please inspect the contents."

The Captain bent over the carton and began pulling out the straw packing. He soon came across a layer of brown paper covered brick looking objects. He looked at Squid and asked, "Son, mind if I borrow your knife?"

Squid replied, "Not at all Captain." He drew his knife out of its sheave and handed it to the Captain.

The Captain slit open one brick down the middle revealing a white chalking power. He looked at Turk and said, "Well I'll be damned. I would bet a million dollars this is cocaine."

Turk reached over and touched his finger on the white powder and licked his finger saying, "Your right, Captain! That's a million dollar find."

Squid and Dawg secured the lid back on the carton and placed it back into the container. After closing the doors to the container the Captain slapped a padlock on it and said, "Nobody is going to open this container again except the Bermuda authorities when we dock.

Turk pulled out his gun and fired several times at the container splattering red and green paint balls all over the side. Turk smiled and said, "The authorities won't have any trouble finding this container." Turk added, "With your permission, Captain, we'll inspect the rest of your shipment."

The Captain replied, "Permission granted."

From the dark corner of the hold the concealed crewmember had been whispering to his boss MÁXIMO what had been happening. MÁXIMO was furious. He screamed through the phone, "Kill them all! I'm not going to lose another shipment."

The phone call went dead. The drug smuggler knew what had to be done. He stepped out of the darkness and began firing his weapon in the direction of Turk, his crew and the Captain. Squid was hit in the leg and dropped to the deck. Saber grabbed him and quickly pulled him aside out of the line of fire and began administering medical attention to him.

Meanwhile in rapid succession Turk and his crew were firing paint balls at the smuggler. The stinging hits from the exploding paint balls were very distracting. Not to mention he was almost blinded. Dawg knew that the smuggler was not about to quit firing his weapon no matter how many times he was hit. He pulled out his boning knife and threw it at the smuggler striking him in the chest. The smuggler screamed and fell back into the darkness and vanished.

Turk yelled out, "Mulate, help Saber tend to Squid. Dawg come with me and let's get that bastard." Turk and Dawg ran after the smuggler, but the area around the containers was pitch black. After searching in vain for several minutes Turk grabbed Dawg by the shoulder and said, "Where the bloody hell did he go?"

Dawg replied, "Maybe he went topside."

Dawg was right, MÁXIMO's goon was on the deck leaning over the ships rail in agony talking to his boss on the GPS phone. The goon had told MÁXIMO everything that had just happened including the run in with the vigilantes. He even described the Phantom to MÁXIMO from his position looking over the ships rail. MÁXIMO had heard enough, he was pissed off and began screaming over the phone, "You idiot. You just cost me millions of dollars. When I find you, you're a dead man, amigo!"

Without saying another word, the goon took the phone away from his ear and dropped it into the ocean. By now Turk and Dawg came busting through a nearby hatch. The goon looked in the direction of Turk and Dawg and said, "Adios, amigo." He lifted his pistol to his temple and pulled the trigger. Turk tried in vain to stop him by waving his arms, but he was too late. The blast from the gun resonated across the ship's deck. The goon's limp body simply rolled over the ship's rail and fell into the black night. A second later a splash was heard and then dead silence. Turk and Dawg made their way to the rail, but there was nothing to see. Turk pounded his fist on the rail and yelled out, "Dawg, we were so close. I know we could have made him spill his guts out and tell us who his boss was. Now we've got nothing, but a drug seizure."

Dawg replied, "Well boss, no matter what, it's still one hell of a drug bust."

Turk added, "I know." The two men turned around walking back to the hatch door to check on Squid.

CHAPTER 10

Columbia Bounty Hunters

COLUMBIA BOUNTY HUNTERS

MÁXIMO was beside himself. Never in his life had someone else taken so much away from him. To make matters worse he didn't even know who it was. All he had was a description of a ship and the name of the ship. His goon had also thought that he had heard a Bermudian accent. It was not much to go on, but that's all he had.

A few days later a pair of Columbian bounty hunters showed up at MÁXIMO's Cuban fortress. The two bounty hunters were escorted to MÁXIMO's study where he had been awaiting their arrival. As they entered the room MÁXIMO laid his cigar down in an ashtray on his desk and briskly walked over to the pair giving each of them a hug. MÁXIMO started the conversation by saying, "Welcome to my humble home. I am MÁXIMO, have a seat and tell me about yourselves." MÁXIMO picked up his cigar and leaned against his desk waiting for the bounty hunters to sit down. MÁXIMO continued on by saying, "And who do I have the pleasure of meeting?"

One of the bounty hunters replied, "We have no names, MÁXIMO. It is our way. We are here to provide our services and nothing more." The other bounty hunter nodded his head in agreement.

MÁXIMO laughed and said, "Well, mister no name, let's just get down to business."

The bounty hunter gestured with his hand for MÁXIMO to continue. MÁXIMO continued to say, "I have already given you everything I know about these thieving bastards who have stolen millions of dollars from me over the last few months. Have your sources come up with any new information?"

The second bounty hunter replied, "Even with our connections we have been able to obtain very little information on these people."

MÁXIMO added, "Tell me what you have."

The second bounty hunter continued, "We don't think they're any type of a government strike force. They're too unpredictable and don't follow typical government agency protocol. In other words, they are hired guns like us or vigilantes. Our inside sources find no trace of their presence anywhere in the United States, and we have excellent informants in Miami. So for now we will assume your associate having heard the Bermudian accent was correct, and we will scour the waters around Bermuda until we find something."

MÁXIMO added, "Very good, my friends. Make sure you thank my associates in Columbia for providing me with your services."

The first bounty hunter replied, "Not a problem, you have paid us well. Besides, even your associates in Columbia have lost shipments to these phantoms." The two bounty hunters stood up and shook MÁXIMO's hand as they turned to walk towards the door.

MÁXIMO shouted out, "Amigo, wait just a minute. Can Benito and his men assist you?"

The two bounty hunters stopped in their tracks and turned back facing MÁXIMO. One bounty hunter replied, "No, amigo, we work alone.

MÁXIMO pounded his fist on his desk and screamed, "When you find those bastards do whatever you want to them, but bring them to me alive even if it's just barely alive. I will cut their hearts out while they take their last breath. Now go!"

The two turned back around and walked out the door. MÁXIMO sat down at his desk, drank a shot of tequila and took a draw on his Cuban cigar. He was content to wait for the bounty hunters to return with their prisoners. He knew these Columbian bounty hunters had been executing enemies of the Columbian drug lords for years. These Bermudians, or whoever they were, would be no exception.

Meanwhile in the dark of the night, The Phantom cruised back into Bermuda. Squid needed medical attention for his gunshot wound. Not to draw attention to the band of marauders, a trusted hospital surgeon was brought to the Morgan's Point complex to remove the bullet. After the surgery was over Turk went to visit Squid in his room on the ship. Turk walked into Squid's room where he found Squid on the top bunk and Mugger on the bottom bunk snoring away like nothing had happened. Turk laid one hand on Squid's bunk and asked, "Well, mate, does your recuperating accommodations meet with your approval?"

Squid leaned over the rail of the bunk bed and pointed down to the bunk below saying, "If that big oaf would quit snoring maybe I could get some rest."

Turk smiled and replied, "Not a problem, mate." Turk picked up his left foot and lightly nudged Mugger's big belly. Mugger wiggled his body then rolled over on his side trying to ignore Turk. Almost instantly all went quiet. Turk smiled again at Squid and said, "See mate, instant quiet. Now get some rest. We'll be back on the open seas in a couple of days, and I need you."

In a great deal of pain, Suid sat up on his elbows and said, "Not to worry, Captain, I'll be ready."

Turk gave Squid a pat on the shoulder and said, "Excellent. I'll be back to check on you tomorrow." Turk turned away leaving the room and made his way towards the bridge.

As Turk entered the bridge he found Bucko and Dawg sipping on a couple of bottles of beer. Turk yelled out, "Did anyone give you two sea scum permission to have alcohol on the bridge?"

Dawg jumped up out of his chair and yelled back, "No sir, Captain."

Turk replied, " What now, Bucko? Should we have him walk the plank or put him in chains strung up to the yardarm?"

Bucko stood up saying, "Captain, permission to have a beer on the bridge please."

Turk laughed and added, "Permission granted, you old sea dogs. Where's my bloody beer?"

Bucko reached over and grabbed one out of the cooler and handed it to Turk.

Turk took the beer. He took a large swallow, wiped his mouth with his coat sleeve and said, "Thanks, mates, I needed that." He went on saying, "Do you two feel up to a trip to Court Street to check out the state of the local drug business? "

Bucko asked, "Captain, don't you think that will be a bloody mistake? After all we're not exactly their favorite cousins. What about Inspector Savage? If he finds out we've been down on Court Street he'll lock us up in Westgate prison."

Turk barked back, "Look damn it. Right now the dope dealers will think we're one of them. Besides I want to find out if we're drying up their supply line."

Bucko replied, 'You better be right, mate, or we might be someone's shark bait tomorrow."

Dawg jumped into the conversation adding. "This sounds like my kind of trip. When do we get going? I've got your back, man."

Turk smiled and said, "Come on, you scum buckets. Let's go visit our friends before I change my mind." Turk walked off the bridge with Bucko and Dawg not far behind.

CHAPTER 11

The Dark Side of Court Street

THE DARK SIDE OF COURT STREET

It was about ten pm when the three left the ship. No sooner had they climbed into Turk's jeep, when a figure came running out of the darkness. It was Jawz. He jumped into the back of the jeep and yelled out, "Dawg, move your big butt over and make room for me. I don't want to miss out on this party."

A bit annoyed, Turk said, "What the bloody hell are you doing here, Jawz? There's no party. We're just going for a short ride, mate."

Jawz snapped back, "Sure you are. I heard you were going down to Court Street to check out the action."

Turk replied, "We are, but so what?"

Jawz added, "What the hell do you think you're going to find out on Court Street with two white boys tagging along?"

Bucko turned to Turk and added, "He's right, Turk."

Turk snapped back, "Alright. Point taken. Hang on." He slapped the gear shift in first and floored the gas pedal. The jeep spun out sideways and shot down the road like a bat out of hell.

The late night drive into Hamilton took Turk and his crew about fifteen minutes. Turk elected to park on nearby Victoria Street. His plan was to go on foot to where the action was. He felt by walking they might be less conspicuous. The four were quick to jump out of the jeep and began walking towards Court Street. After a short walk Turk turned to the others and said, "Look, mates, we ought to split up. Bucko, you stick with me. We'll go see if some of my old snitches are still hanging out at the Black Dragon Club. Jawz, you and Dawg take a stroll down Court Street and see what the buzz is about." Turk and Bucko turned around and walked over to Union Street while Jawz and Dawg continued on to Court Street.

A few minutes later Turk and Bucko made their way to the Black Dragon on Dundonald Street. Just as Turk was about to walk through the door, Bucko reached out and grabbed Turk by the shoulder stopping him dead in his tracks. Turk turned back and snapped, "What the bloody hell is the matter?"

Bucko let go of Turk saying, "Mate, are you sure you want to go in there? You might be biting off more than you can chew."

Turk smiled and said, "Not to worry, old friend. I'm hungry, plus a cold Heineken will hit the spot." The two laughed and walked through the doorway one after the other.

Meanwhile Jawz and Dawg had made their way down a couple of blocks on Court Street. The first block was fairly quiet and isolated to shop traffic. Halfway down the second block the pair ran into an old school mate of Jawz. Jawz reached out his hand for a brothers hand shake and said, "My man, where in the hell have you been hanging out?"

Jawz old school mate replied, "You know— just the same old gig."

Jawz replied, "Man, I've been out to sea forever. What's the word on the street for a brother and his friend to score?"

The smile on the brother left and he snapped back, "First of all, I don't shoot up anything and I'm pissed off that you think I do. What the hell is the matter with you, man? I work my ass off on the streets trying to keep kids clean, and my old friend is down here trying to score dope."

He paused for a few seconds and continued, "Thank God, the word on the street is the supply is drying up." He started to leave and suddenly turned back to say, "Jawz, if I see you on this street again I may just have to kick your ass."

As the brother walked off Jawz raised his arm and was about to say something when Dawg pulled his arm back and said, "Let him go. He told us what we wanted to know. When this is all over you make amends with him."

Jawz with his head hung low said, "Man, do I feel bad. Here's a brother trying to do the right thing, risking his life, and here I'm adding grief to his life."

Dawg replied, "Someday he'll know what this was all about." Jawz nodded his head and the two continued on down the street.

Back in the Black Dragon Turk and Bucko made their way over to the bar and sat down. The bartender walked over to Turk and Bucko and asked, "Do you two dead-beats really want a drink in this joint?"

Turk smiled saying, "You're damn right, barkeep. Give us two cold ones."

The bartender grabbed the first two bottles of beer out of the cooler, popped them open and slammed them down on the bar. Foam spewed out of the bottles like the geyser "Old Faithful". He walked off without saying a word.

Bucko and Turk clicked their bottles of beer together. Bucko said, "Cheers to the most friendly bar in Bermuda."

Turk laughed and added, "Well, what the hell do you expect, mate? We're not exactly their cup of tea."

A few seconds later Turk felt a very large hand on his shoulder. He turned around and looked up at the outline of a very large man. Turk asked, "Mate, what can I do for you?"

The big man replied, "Don't you remember me, Detective Black?"

Bucko knew this was not going to be pretty. He was sure Turk must have busted this man in years past, but for the life of him he couldn't remember him. Still looking up at him, Turk said, "Yeah mate, aren't you in my Sunday school class?"

The big man was getting really annoyed. He reached down with both hands to grab Turk by the collar, but before he could Turk elbowed him in the groin. The big man bent over in agony. Without wasting a second Turk grabbed him by his head and slammed it on the bar. After the impact, the big man fell over backwards and was out cold on the floor.

Turk reached into his pocket pulled out a bill and dropped it on the bar. He turned to Bucko and said, "Mate, drink up. We just wore out our welcome here."

Bucko starting chugging his beer as fast as he could. All he could think of was, "What 's going to happen?" What was Turk's acquaintance going to do when he woke up? Bucko finally spoke up as he slammed his beer bottle down on the bar, "Man, I'm ready to go." He stood up and started walking towards the door.

Turk yelled out, "Wait just a bloody minute. Give me a hand. I want to take this bum out back and teach him a real lesson."

Bucko walked over and helped Turk pick the big man up off the floor. While they were carrying him towards the back door, Bucko whispered, "Are you crazy, mate? When this guy wakes up, he's going to kill us. And if he doesn't, his friends in the bar will."

As they got outside of the bar and around the corner in the alley Turk said, "Be cool, mate, those bastards in the bar aren't about to step outside." He turned to the big man who was now leaning against the wall and said, "What the hell do you think, Big Bubba?"

Big Bubba looked up and replied, "I think you're both dead men." Bucko just about pissed his pants. Big Bubba and Turk both laughed for a few seconds, then Big Bubba gave Turk a hug. Big Bubba added, "I see, Turk, you can still fake that elbow and slam move as good as ever."

Turk looked at Bucko and said, "Bucko, I want you to meet my old friend, Big Bubba. We used to be acquaintances in my old police days."

Big Bubba shook Bucko's hand and said, "What Turk really meant to say was that I used to be his snitch. " He then turned back to Turk and said, "I thought you got busted. Are you the snitch now, old buddy?"

Turk laughed and replied, "Hell no, my friend. I just need to know what the supply on the street is like these days."

Big Bubba replied, "Supply is down, and prices are up. I think the local dealers are getting nervous. I hear there are some South American Mafia thugs coming to the island to get the drugs flowing again." He looked at Turk and asked, "Mate, you don't have something to do with this do you?"

Turk shook his head and said, "Hell no, mate! The drug goons and the cops both have it in for me." Turk gave Big Bubba a brothers hand shake and added, "We better get the hell out of here before someone does kick our ass, Bucko." The two left Big Bubba and walked around the building to Dundonald Street. From there they walked over to Court Street looking for Dawg and Jawz.

While they walked Bucko said, "You bastard. You scared the hell out of me back at the Black Dragon. I didn't think we were going to leave there alive.

Turk smiled and said, "Not to worry, mate. The plan was in place."

Bucko snapped back, "Yeah, yeah, next time I'll kick your ass." Both men laughed as they continued on to Court Street.

Meanwhile Dawg and Jawz had walked into a local teen gang called the "Razors". Before they knew it the Razors had them surrounded. The ring leader stepped into the circle and confronted Jawz. He said, "What the hell are you and the white boy doing in Razor territory?"

Jawz replied, "Look man, we're just out for a walk. No harm done. Let us pass." Dawg had noticed one of the boys was acting like he was packing under his t-shirt. Dawg nudged Jawz in the side so he would see what was going on. Before anything could escalate Turk and Bucko had made their way down the street and joined the confrontation.

Bucko said, "Oh, marvelous ! We just went from the frying pan into the fire."

The gang leader pulled out a pocket knife and yelled out, "Teach these trespassers a lesson." But before anything could happen police sirens sounded from all directions. Within seconds the cops had the group surrounded. The Razors cut loose in all directions.

Dawg looked over at the gang member who had something under his shirt and tripped him before he could get away. He fell and hit the ground rolling and a small hand gun skidded across the sidewalk. Dawg walked over and picked up the hand gun and yelled at the young man, "Get the hell out of here. If I ever see you with a hand gun again I'll take you out to sea and dump your ass in the ocean." The young man got to his feet and vanished in a second.

Turk heard a familiar voice yelling at them. It was Inspector Savage. He stepped out of the police car and walked straight over to Turk and said, "What in the bloody hell are you doing on Court Street?" Before Turk could answer Savage began yelling, "You've got thirty seconds to get your butts out of here or your next stop is Westgate's."

Turk was pissed. He knew what he had done had been a gamble, but he found out their mission was working and that they would have to be more careful in the future. Turk yelled to his men, "Come on, mates. These bloody coppers mean what they say."

Three of the men walked back the way they came from except for Dawg. He turned around and walked over to Savage and said, "I found this on the sidewalk. I thought you might want it." He handed Savage the small pistol. Before Savage could say anything Dawg broke out in a dead run catching up with the others.

Savage just stood there in the street shaking his head as Turk and his men walked off. Savage turned to his other officers and said, "What the hell are you all staring at? Get back in the cars, and let's head back to the station. Court Street was silent for a few minutes. After Savage and the patrol cars left the area, the streets filled up with people like nothing had ever happened.

CHAPTER 12

Ambushed in the Triangle

AMBUSHED IN THE TRIANGLE

A few days later the Phantom was re-stocked with supplies and weapons and even Squid was on the mend enough to make the voyage. In the dead of the night under a half moon, the Phantom with her electric turbine engines running cruised through The Great Sound in stealth mode. Turk, Squid and Saber had bridge duty that night. Because Squid was not fit for any of the regular demanding duties on the ship, he was relegated to bridge duty and galley duty. Saber had moved out to the railing that surrounded the bridge with a pair of binoculars watching the Sound for any unexpected boat traffic. The slight breeze in the night air left her dark silky hair gently floating in the air. Turk was mesmerized by watching her slender silhouette against the light of the half moon. Suddenly, a deafening scream came from Saber, "Captain, turn starboard! You're about to hit a channel marker."

Turk just about jumped out of his skin as he cranked the wheel as hard as he could. The Phantom missed the large channel marker by inches. Squid stared at Turk for a minute and said with a snicker, "Captain, I know the scenery out in the sound tonight is bloody distracting; but for the safety of the crew, don't you think you should keep your one good eye on the channel?'

Turk exploded yelling, "You sawed off little bastard! You better shut up or the rest of this voyage for you will be washing dishes in the galley." Squid laughed and took a glance through the bridge window at Saber. He could tell Saber was a little embarrassed. However, the smile she had on her face told the real story. Not another word was said on the bridge while the Phantom cruised its way out of the Great Sound and into the open ocean.

The trip south over the next few days had been very quiet. Turk was beginning to be concerned that the drug smugglers were avoiding the waters of the Bermuda Triangle. Although he did not know it at the time, he was not far off in his thought process. Another day went by with no sightings of suspicious ocean going traffic. Meanwhile Turk and most of the crew were having an early morning breakfast in the galley. The small talk of the crew while eating breakfast was drowned out by a call over the ship intercom by Bucko, "Captain to the bridge. We've got a sighting on radar that you ought to see."

Turk jumped up from his bench, tapping Mulate on the back. As he ran for the hatch door he yelled, "Mulate, you come with me. The rest of you finish your breakfast." Turk made his way up to the stairs with Mulate close behind him.

As the two men made their way into the bridge, Bucko waved his arm saying, "Captain, check this out and tell me what the hell you think it is."

Turk looked at the radar screen and said in a puzzled voice, "This object is too narrow to be a ship, but it's also too damn long to be a yacht or a sail boat."

Mulate scratched his head and said, "Mon, do you think it's a submarine?"

Turk replied, "I don't think so. Look how bloody fast it's moving."

Bucko added, "You've got that right. Whatever the hell it is, it's going to be on top of us in less than a minute."

Turk snapped back, "Why in the hell didn't we see this image a long time ago?"

Bucko replied, "The ship, or whatever it is, must have some type of radar blocker onboard. Our system evidently just cracked their blocking signal."

Turk grabbed the intercom mike, flipped the ship's siren and yelled out, "Hands on deck; man your stations." The radar screen began flashing red indicating an impact in less than thirty seconds.

Bucko moved back to the ship's controls and yelled, "Permission to take evasive action, Captain."

Turk looked at the radar screen once more, and just as he was going to reply, the object on the radar screen split into four smaller objects. One object remained on a collision course while the other three veered off in other directions. Turk yelled out over the intercom, "It's a bloody trap! We're about to be hit from all sides."

Turk was right. The bounty hunters from Columbia had been concealing their attack boats by making them look like a single boat to anyone watching them on radar. Their plan was simple. They would surround the Phantom and attack the ship from all sides.

Before the crew from the Phantom could man their weapon systems the Columbian's high speed attack boats were firing machine gun blasts at the Phantom at will. Dawg screamed out, "I know what Custer must have felt like at the battle of the "Little Bighorn."

The Columbians were well equipped. Their arsenal included machine guns, grenade launchers, and shoulder rockets. The Phantom was about to feel the full force of these South American killers. The Phantom took the first hit on her port side from a grenade. To make matters worse the grenade landed next to one of the depth charge canisters. The massive explosion blew a three foot hole in the side of the ship and the deck. Jawz was the only crew member on the port side of the ship when the explosion took place. Saber screamed out, "Man overboard" as she watched Jawz being blown off the deck and into the ocean. Saber and Squid ran to the stern of the ship ducking the machine gun fire to get a life preserver to throw to Jawz.

Meanwhile Turk had taken over control of the ship from Bucko and was trying to take evasive action to save the Phantom from being sunk. He turned the Phantom as hard as to could to the port side and yelled to Bucko, "Launch a depth charge off the starboard side now!" Bucko didn't hesitate. He slammed his fist on the release lever launching the depth charge. The depth charge flew through the air and landed directly in the middle of the deck on the lead attack boat. Because of the sudden impact with the boat, the depth charge exploded instantly. The entire boat was engulfed in flames, and a few seconds later it exploded into a million pieces.

Gunner had made his way to the bow of the ship and was manning the Gatling gun. He turned the gun to the starboard side of the ship and almost immediately began firing thousands of rounds into the attack boat coming from that direction. The attack boat was rendered useless in less than a minute with the entire crew lying dead on her deck. Just as Gunner was about to turn the gun to the port side of the ship his Gatling gun was struck by a rocket fired from a shoulder rocket launcher. Gunner never knew what hit him. Turk saw the rocket strike and the next second Gunner and the Gatling gun had vanished from the deck. Only part of the base of the gun that was bolted down was still visible.

Turk yelled out, "Mulate, take the wheel. I've got to stop those bastards off the port side before they fire another rocket at us." Mulate grabbed the wheel while Turk ran for the bridge hatch. As he went through the hatch he reached up and removed a M16 rifle that was mounted above the hatch. A Columbian was within seconds of firing another rocket at the Phantom.

As soon as Turk cleared the hatch door be dropped to one knee and fired off the entire clip at the Columbian. The Columbian's entire body shook from the multiple hits from the M16 bullets ripping through his body. As the Columbian fell backwards his rocket launched, but to the dismay of his fellow crew members the rocket fired through the windshield of his own boat and exploded on impact. The attack boat split in half and began sinking.

The last Columbian attack boat was now in position behind the Phantom and they had abruptly reconsidered their attack strategy. A hasty retreat now seemed their only recourse. The attack boat spun about and went full throttle on a southerly course.

Squid saw their retreat and yelled out, "They're making a run for it."

Turk stepped back through the hatch door and said, "Mulate, let's catch up to that boat. I don't want them to get away. I want to find out who's responsible for this ambush." He then turned to Bucko and added, "As soon as we get within five hundred yards of those bastards I want you to train one of our rockets on their rear engines. I want that boat dead in the water."

Bucko replied, "Roger that, Captain." The Phantom was now closing in on five hundred yards of the attack boat. No matter how hard the Columbians tried to outrun the Phantom it just wasn't going to happen. The Phantom could outrun any ocean going vessel anywhere. Bucko spoke up, "Captain, we're locked in on the boat. Permission to fire."

Turk nodded his head and said, "Damn it, just fire the bloody rocket!"

Bucko flipped the firing switch. The rocket blasted out of its launcher in a split second. Seconds later the rocket scored a direct hit on the stern of the attack boat. Both props on the boat were destroyed. The attack boat was dead in the water. Turk walked to the bow of the ship with a megaphone. Turk lifted the megaphone to his mouth and said, "Mates, you have three minutes to toss all your weapons overboard or I'll blow you and your boat to hell and back." He turned facing the bridge and said, "Turn this lady around, and let's go back and pull Jawz out of the brink before he becomes shark bait."

There was no hesitation from the bridge. The Phantom trolled back through the battle scarred waters making sure they didn't run over Jawz. The entire crew leaned over the gun rails of the ship keeping a lookout for Jawz. Finally Mugger yelled out, "I see him, I see him." He pointed off to the starboard side of the ship. Even before Bucko could bring the ship around Mugger and Squid dove into the water to rescue Jawz. As they neared Jawz he began paddling with his one free arm towards his two friends. By the time the three hooked up with each other the Phantom had pulled alongside. Jawz was alive, but pretty beat up. Mugger and Squid helped lift him up to the others on deck. While Saber tended to Jawz, Turk spoke to the entire crew saying, "Today we lost a good friend and a tireless member of the crew. We all knew when we signed on to the Phantom the risks were great, but this war on drugs has to be fought and won. Gunner knew the risks and believed in our cause. We will never forget our mate." Turk bowed his head in silent prayer with the others for a minute.

Turk added, "Mulate and Mugger help Saber get Jawz below deck." He turned to the rest of the crew and said, "Men, this is just the beginning. We've inflicted damage on these drug smugglers and they are mad as hell now and they've just proved they're not going down without a fight. Man your stations, and let's find out who these bastards are. I want to know who in the bloody hell wants to kill us."

As the crew went to their stations Bucko yelled out, "If they pull a weapon out on me I'll blow their brains out." A few minutes later the Phantom pulled alongside of what was left of the attack boat. The crew of the Phantom had their weapons trained on the three surviving members of the crew.

Turk yelled out, "Place your hands behind you head and keep them there. We're coming aboard and if any of you even blink we will shoot first and ask questions later."

The Columbians complied with Turk's demand. Turk, Mugger, Dawg and Squid went aboard the attack boat. Turk looked at the three Columbians and asked, "What's this all about? Why did you thugs attack us?" There was silence for a moment. Turk interrupted the silence yelling, "Do you speak English mates?"

Finally, one of the Columbians stepped forward. He was one of the men who had visited MÁXIMO in Cuba. In a very low tone he said, "We were sent here to kill the ghosts who keep stealing our property."

Turk snapped back, "Look mate we're not stealing, but we're stopping drug smuggling scum like you from bringing illegal drugs into Bermuda and the US. Now tell me this, and you better tell the truth or I'll throw you all overboard to the sharks. Who the bloody hell is we?"

The Columbian shook his head and did not answer. Turk looked over at Mugger and winked with his one good eye. He barked out, "Mugger, throw one of these scum buckets overboard."

Mugger didn't say a word; he grabbed one of the Columbians by the collar and lifted him over his head. As he walked over to the gunwhale of the boat the Columbian bounty hunter spoke up, "Put him down. Yes, we are Columbian bounty hunters, but it was Zorra MÁXIMO, drug lord of Cuba, who sent us to kill you. The Cubans are very pissed off at you right now. They want you dead."

Turk replied, "Well, that's just too damn bad." He turned to Mugger and said, "Put the man down." He went on to say, "Destroy all of their communications equipment and search them for cell phones. We'll leave them for the authorities." He looked over at the Phantom and added, "Bucko, get some food and water, we don't want these bloody killers to die on the open sea." Turk handed to the Columbian a small GPS device and said, "Mate, keep this and the authorities will find your bloody butts. Lose it overboard, and you're just another boat lost in the Bermuda Triangle." Turk turned and stepped back on the Phantom. The crew untied the attack boat from the Phantom and continued on their original southerly route.

As the Columbian lost sight of the Phantom he looked at the tracking device Turk had given him. He yelled out, "Revenge will be ours, you cowards." He threw the device in the ocean in the direction from where he had last seen the Phantom.

CHAPTER 13

The Lines are Drawn

THE LINES ARE DRAWN

Later that night in the ship's galley the entire crew met to discuss the day's events. Normally, Turk would have someone on watch in the bridge, but tonight he had the Phantom on automatic pilot. They were miles away from the Columbian attack boat and outside of the standard shipping lanes. Even though the Phantom had suffered extensive damage earlier in the day Turk felt the crew needed to be together.

Turk entered the galley somewhat later than the rest of the crew. He sat down while Mugger passed him a beer. After a couple of drinks Turk said, "Mates, I have gathered some interesting information about the sponsor of today's attack. If the Columbian told the truth, and it was MÁXIMO, then we're in for some big challenges."

Dawg slammed his beer down on the table and said, "What's so special about this drug king pin?"

Turk went on to say, "For one thing, mate, he's under the unofficial protection of the Cuban government. He must be giving the cash strapped government payoffs for protection. He makes the Columbians look like school kids when it comes to drug trafficking. He's a vicious killer and he will stop at nothing to get what he wants."

Bucko asked, "Is there more?"

Turk replied, "Oh yeah, to make matters worse, Cuba is just outside of the Bermuda Triangle."

Jawz said, "So what does that matter?"

Turk replied, "Our bloody Letter of Marque only protects us in the waters of the Bermuda Triangle. So if we go after this bastard we're on our own. His operation is somewhere in the vicinity of Guantánamo Bay."

Dawg spoke up, "Good, I have some navy buddies stationed there."

Turk added, "That's a nice thought Dawg, but unless they want to create an international incident we're on our own. If and when we go after MÁXIMO there will be no help mates." He raised his beer in the air and said, "Cheers to the Phantom and her crew." The crew tapped their bottles together.

Meanwhile back in Cuba MÁXIMO was waiting anxiously for the Columbians to arrive with news from Bermuda. To his surprise only one Columbian walked through the door into his study. Making matters worse MÁXIMO had never seen this man before. MÁXIMO stood up from his chair and with a deep voice said, "Amigo, who the hell are you, and where are my bounty hunter friends?"

The Columbian replied, "They are no more, MÁXIMO."

Before he could say another word MÁXIMO yelled out, "You are not my contact. You're not allowed to address me by my name. Amigo, you do that again, and I'll kill you!" MÁXIMO pulled out a small automatic pistol from under his desk and laid it on its side. He added, "Continue on with your report, amigo."

The Columbian was now very nervous. However, he continued with his report, "Yesterday four of our attack boats made a surprise attack on what we believe was a Bermudian stealth ship. The Bermudian ship took heavy damage from our attack boats. We know that at least two of our attack boats were destroyed, but since then we have had no contact with our men."

MÁXIMO picked up the pistol pointing it at the Columbian and yelled, "Amigo, do you think I'm stupid? Bermuda has no navy much less a ship of any kind. My patience is running thin."

The Columbian added, "This is some type of vigilante group trying to wreck havoc on our drug business."

MÁXIMO replied, "I think they're doing a damn good job of it."

The Columbian continued, "We have decided to cut our losses and pull out of this hunt. We're very uncomfortable dealing with this unpredictable situation. This is no longer our war. Our union is dissolved." He turned and walked towards the door.

MÁXIMO stood up and yelled, "You're right, amigo. This is the end of our union." He reached down and picked up the pistol firing it at the back of the Columbian. The Columbian was hit multiple times in the back. He hit the floor with a thud while his blood spurted in all directions. MÁXIMO walked over to the dead Columbian and said, "We'll handle the Bermudians, amigo." MÁXIMO stepped over the lifeless body and left the study. He was not going to let any vigilantes get in the way of his drug distribution business. This was war, and he knew his friends in the Cuba military owed him many favors. He would find what he needed to destroy the Bermudians.

CHAPTER 14

Secret of the Gold Coast

SECRET OF THE GOLD COAST

As the Phantom made her way south Turk and Bucko had determined that with a three foot diameter hole in her side the Phantom's seaworthiness might be in question. The turbulent waters of the Bermuda Triangle are not very forgiving especially with a damaged ship. The Phantom also needed refitting for her lost weapon systems. None of this could be accomplished in Bermuda. The repairs must be done at a secret naval base in Florida. This is one of only a few bases in the world that has the technological capabilities to service a stealth ship.

Turk, Bucko, and Mulate were all on the bridge as the Phantom headed westerly towards the gold coast of Florida. Mulate had taken over the ship's wheel while Turk went over to sit down in the captain's chair. Bucko was trying to relax by lying down on top of the map table.

While Mulate was at the ship's wheel he turned to Turk and asked, "What are the coordinates for this military ship yard we're going to?"

Turk smiled and replied, "It beats the bloody hell out of me."

Mulate, being the ship's navigator, said with a puzzled look on his face, "Look mon, the Gold Coast is one big area. Are we going to cruise up and down the coast until they spot us?"

Turk added, "Chill out mate, you'll figure it out soon enough."

It was only fifteen minutes later, when Mulate was fairly relaxed at the ship's wheel that the wheel began turning right then left as if it were on autopilot. Mulate jumped back from the wheel screaming, "Look mon, a ghost has taken over the ship."

Turk jumped up abruptly awakened from his nap. He saw what was going on and began laughing.

Mulate looked at Turk and said, "What the hell is so damn funny, mon?"

Turk replied, "Mate, you just got your first taste of the ship's automatic guidance system. Don't worry. We won't be going anywhere until it gets dark. The US Navy doesn't even want us to know where we're going. Right now they're just testing out our systems. Mulate, you might as well go below deck and rest for awhile. It looks like our job on the bridge is done for the time being."

Mulate started walking around the bridge like a chicken with its head cut off. Bucko sat up on the map table and grabbed Mulate as he walked by. He asked, "Mulate, what in the hell is the matter with you? Sit down and relax."

Mulate snapped back, "Mon, there is no way in hell I'm missing this action. There's no telling where we're going, and I can't let anything happen to the Phantom. What if a cargo ship crosses our path? Then what, we gonna sink?"

Turk smiled and added, "Mulate, you do what you gotta do, mate. I'm going to sit back and enjoy the ride." Turk leaned back in his captain's chair and said, "If we're off duty, Bucko, grab us a couple of cold ones."

Bucko replied, "Roger that, Captain." He jumped off the map table and walked over to a small cooler on the floor. He grabbed a couple of beers and handed one to Turk. The two men clicked their bottles and had a drink.

Meanwhile Mulate was keeping an eye on all the controls and screening the waters for other ships. As the sun sank below the horizon the ships engines fired up and the navigation equipment started working. Mulate yelled out, " We're moving, mon. Now I'll be able to plot our course and figure out the location of our secret destination." Just as he finished speaking all the navigational instruments went blank. Mulate looked mystified. He asked, "What the hell just happened? All the electronics just went dead, but the Phantom is still on some directional plan, and the engines are still running."

Turk spoke up, "What the bloody blue blazes do you think, Mulate? If we're going to a secret location, do you think the US Navy wants us to figure out where we're going so that someday we might tell others? I think not, mate."

Mulate was disappointed, but he understood. He left the bridge, went to the bow of the ship, leaned on the gun rail and just stared out into the blackness of the night wondering where they were going.

Several hours had passed since the Phantom had gone on the autopilot system. An hour or so earlier Saber had joined Mulate on the bow of the deck waiting for the coastline to show. They didn't have to wait long. Through a light fog they were able to see faint lights off in the distance. This surely meant that the navy base was not far away.

Saber entered the bridge, walked over to Turk, shook his shoulder and whispered into his ear, "Are you ready for breakfast in bed, Captain?" Turk slowly opened his eyes with a grin from ear to ear. Before Turk could say anything Saber smiled and said, "Get that thought out of your mind. I think you might want to call the crew. It looks like we're close to land."

Turk stood up and went over to the ship's intercom and said, "All hands on deck. Land ho." One after another the crew made their way from below deck. Another hour passed, but they could tell they were entering a fairly narrow channel. The further into the channel they motored it was obvious they were now being watched from both shorelines by navy MP's holding automatic weapons. Jawz looked over at Dawg and asked, "Are these blokes here to guard us or shoot us?"

Dawg replied, "Looks to me like there here to protect the Phantom. They could probably care less about us."

After about thirty minutes in the channel the Phantom entered a small bay. Halfway across the bay a huge steel docking bay rose from beneath the water. The docking bay was fully enclosed except for the front of it. It was apparent to the entire crew that the Phantom was about to be swallowed up. Bucko looked over at Turk saying, "Captain, are we really going into that steel crate?"

Also a bit amazed, Turk said, "Well, my good friend, there doesn't appear to be much we can do about it right at the moment."

The Phantom floated slowly into the docking bay. Within two minutes the ship was engulfed entirely inside of the bay. Shortly after that, two large doors closed sealing the Phantom completely inside the docking bay. A few minutes later it was evident that the water was being drained from the dry dock. With a look of concern Bucko asked, "Captain, why the hell are we being sealed in this dry dock like sardines in a can?"

Turk smiled and said, "Well mate, I'm guessing it's because we're about to be submerged and lowered down to a hidden dry dock under the bay."

Bucko snapped back, "I didn't sign up for any bloody submarine duty. I want my feet on land or on the deck of a ship and not in Davy Jones locker."

Turk replied, "Bucko, old boy, it's a little late to be worried now. I suspect we're going to be swimming with the sharks for several days."

Bucko just dropped his head and said, "Oh crap!"

A few minutes later the two felt a huge thump. They could both tell the sardine can had just struck bottom. To their surprise it soon felt like the sardine can was on a rail system rolling across the bottom of the bay.

Another ten minutes passed before the sardine can came to an abrupt halt. After waiting for awhile Turk spoke first, "Bucko, do you think we're stuck on the bottom of the bay or did we make it to the dry dock?"

As the two looked out the bow of the Phantom they could both hear pounding on the door. Next the seals on the vacuum door began separating allowing water to spray through the seals all around the door.

Turk and Bucko just stood there staring at the water blasting through the loose seals. Finally Turk said, "Well mate, this might be the end of the line for us. Whoever sees Davy Jones first put in a good word for the other."

They were just about to get each other a hug when the door sprang open, and a figure stepped into the sardine can yelling out, "What the hell are you morons doing to our ship? We leave it with you for a few months, and you get a hole blown threw her side as big as a football field."

Turk didn't know what to say at first until he could finally see the person step out of the shadows. Turk yelled back, "You old son-of-a- bitch. I left your obnoxious partner in Bermuda and now I have to deal with you. What the hell is going on?"

The man who stepped out of the darkness was none other than Special FBI Agent, Derrick Storm. Storm laughingly added, "If you and your crew hadn't done such a spectacular job over the last few months we might bust all of you for a host of laws you've broken. But enough of that, get your crew off the Phantom while we send a repair crew aboard."

Turk yelled back, "We want to help repair the Phantom."

Storm shook his head in disagreement and added, "Don't worry, my friend. We have plenty to keep you and your crew busy while your ship is being repaired." As he turned around to walk off he yelled back, "Get that crew of misfits and have them follow me now! We don't have much time."

He walked out of the sardine can and was out of sight in minutes.

Turk thought to himself, "You bastard." He picked up the ship's mike and yelled out, "All hands on deck in five minutes. We've got a job to do." Turk slammed the mike down on the table and walked out of the bridge to wait for his crew on the ship's bow.

CHAPTER 15

The Bimini Bust

THE BIMINI BUST

The Phantom's crew found themselves waiting by a helicopter pad back on the surface. Several minutes later, a silhouette of a single Black Hawk helicopter came into view in the late afternoon sky. Saber looked at Storm and said, "Are we going to a party?"

Storm replied, "Not quite, my lady, but you are going to a gathering." Saber and everyone else that could hear Storm all seemed puzzled. Storm went on to say, "I'll fill you all in once we get underway." There wasn't much of a wait. The Black Hawk landed a few minutes later and the Phantom's crew was aboard and back in the air in ten minutes. Storm hand signaled the crew to get their attention. Once the crew had huddled together he spoke, "We're on our way to Miami. From there your mission will be to intercept a huge drug shipment on the coast of North Bimini Island in the Bahamas."

Turk asked, "Why the bloody hell isn't the US or the Bahamian police doing this?"

Storm replied, "We just received this information from a reliable source a few hours ago. Furthermore, about the same time, our eyes on Guantánamo sighted two power boats leaving Cuba on a similar course. The bottom line is neither law enforcement agency has the time or manpower to get the proper paper work together to make this bust stick."

Turk smiled and said, "So you want the Bermuda cowboys to go in and bail your butts out?"

Storm nodded his head in agreement. He went on to say, "This will probably be a huge shipment worth millions. Since the shipment is probably from the drug lord MÁXIMO in Cuba and he won't be onboard, we'll only have small time thugs to prosecute. So let's destroy the drugs while we have a chance and maybe take down a few thugs at the same time. This should really put a dent in his cash flow."

Turk replied, "The blood sucker will really be pissed now."

Storm added, "You're right, Turk. Maybe he'll be so pissed off he'll finally make a fatal mistake."

Turk replied, "Yeah, like trying to kill us."

Storm smiled and said, "Well, I wasn't thinking that, but we'll be ready when he does screw up." Storm could tell the Black Hawk had arrived at their destination. He pointed out the window and said, "Look below, team. We've got a couple of confiscated Stinger speed boats down there waiting for you."

As Turk and the crew unloaded from the Black Hawk, Bucko hesitated before leaving the chopper and turned back to Storm asking, "How the hell are we going to find the rendezvous point on North Bimini?"

Storm replied, "I was hoping someone was going to ask." He pulled out a GPS device and flipped it to Bucko saying, "This will get you there, guys, and if it's not too dark you'll see an old rusted out shipwreck on the shoreline. That's where the exchange is going to take place. Now get your butts out of here before it's too late. Oh, your weapons are under the seats."

Turk, Bucko, Mulate, and Saber went on one Stinger; while Jawz, Squid, Mugger, and Dawg took off in the other Stinger. Turk knew they had to make time. It was late in the afternoon and they would have to cover fifty miles. Hopefully they would get there first, but if the

Bahamians were already there they would love the advantage of a surprise.

Meanwhile the Cuban speed boats were closing in on Bimini. Benito was at the wheel of one of the speed boats with a trusted lieutenant at the wheel of the other speed boat. Benito was under a ton of pressure to make this drug exchange. His boss MÁXIMO was just about at his wits end because of all the losses he had suffered over the last six months. Although they did not know who the attackers were, the Cubans knew they were Bermudians. They also knew their ship had taken severe damage. MÁXIMO was positive that there would be no threat to this drug exchange.

The Cubans were now in cell range with the Bahamas. Benito picked up his cell phone and called Mongol the Bahamian who was making the drug pickup on the shipwreck on the Bimini coast. After several rings Mongol answered, "My brother, are we going to dance tonight?"

Benito only tolerated Mongol because he was a reliable customer; otherwise, he could do without him. After a brief pause Benito replied, "Yes amigo, unless your sister is there."

Mongol added, "No, it's just me. My sister went to another party. The dance floor is open."

Benito replied, "Good, have me a bottle of rum waiting." He then hung up. Benito knew that when Mongol said the dance floor was open it was safe to pull alongside the old wreck. Benito turned to his men and said, "Amigos, we're going in. Lock and load!"

Back on the Stingers Turk had picked up the Cuban boats on the portable radar system. Turk turned to Saber saying, "Let the others know we'll be making contact with the Cubans shortly. Since they're ahead of us the element of surprise will be lost. Be ready to take on enemy fire as soon as we're spotted."

Saber replied, "Roger that, Captain." She picked up the boat radio and called the others on Stinger Two to get ready for action.

Mulate and Bucko lifted up the boat cushions to check out their firepower. Mulate smiled and said, "Not bad for short notice. I see we have M16's, grenade launchers, and armor piercing assault automatic weapons." The crew on the other Stinger found the same arsenal of weapons to use. Saber and Turk picked up M16's; while Mulate took the grenade launcher and Bucko was happy to hoist the assault rifle.

Meanwhile the Cubans were within a mile of the wreck. Since it was now dark their only visual was a beam of light Mongol was shinning from a lantern. Benito called his other boat saying, "When we get within one hundred yards of shore you idle your boat and guard our backside. I don't want any surprises."

The voice on the other end of the call replied, "No problem, boss."

Knowing he had his back covered Benito cautiously made his way to the shipwreck. Once alongside he stepped onto the wreck with two of his men packing AK-47's for protection. Once he saw Mongol and his men step out of the shadows Benito signaled his other men to start unloading the cocaine bricks. After shaking hands with Mongol, Benito said, "Amigo, let me see the money."

Mongol replied, "Sure, man." He slapped his hands together, and one of his men stepped forward with a briefcase. Mongol took it from him and handed it to Benito.

Benito took the case and said, "I'll go count the cash, and you count your bricks and do whatever tests you do." Because the two trusted each other they both turned away and got to work doing what needed to be done.

From the Stinger, Turk had also seen Mongol's light signal to the Cubans. Although it was now pitch black Turk's GPS device had a fix on the shipwreck. Turk had decided to have both Stingers circle around each side of the wreck and attack in a pincher style attack. His plan was to surprise the Cubans from both sides avoiding a frontal attack. This was a good plan since he didn't know if one of the Cuban speed boats could block the way on a frontal attack.

The Stingers idled along at low speed for as long as they could without being heard. They were now within a couple hundred yards of the wreck. Turk knew it was now or never if he was going to catch the Cubans and the Bahamians together. Turk screamed over the radio, "Let's take these bad asses out!" Just as Turk finished speaking both Stingers were fully throttled and blasted across the water. A few seconds later the crew on both Stingers began firing everything they had at the wreck.

Benito started screaming, "It's a trap. Kill the Bahamians." His men started shooting at Mongol and his men.

Mongol yelled out, "Don't shoot! We're cool!" But before he could finish a bullet struck him in the throat. Blood spewed everywhere. Mongol tripped backwards and fell through an opening in the rusted out flooring of the ship.

The Cubans now turned their firepower in the direction of the two Stingers. Benito screamed out, "It must be those bastards from Bermuda. Kill them all!"

The two Stingers were laying down such a simultaneous firing line that the Cubans and Bahamians could hardly get a shot off.

From Stinger Two Dawg fired off his grenade launcher and made a direct hit on one Cuban speed boat. Mugger looked at Dawg and said, "That drug smuggling boat won't be going anywhere anytime soon.

No sooner had Mugger spoken than the second Cuban boat came up on the starboard side of Stinger Two blasting the boat with multiple AK-47's. Mugger reacted and tried to turn around, but before he could his back was riddled with bullets fired from the Cubans. Mugger's entire body shook violently and he fell overboard in the black darkness of the ocean. Squid took control of the Stinger and veered the boat in the opposite direction of the Cuban speed boat.

Meanwhile Turk and his Stinger made another pass at the Cuban boat still tied up to the old wreck. As they passed the boat, Turk fired their entire arsenal at it. The boat was now on fire, sinking quickly, and most of the bricks of cocaine were now dust in the wind. Benito and two of his thugs had jumped overboard with the money before the boat caught fire. It was soon evident to Benito that the briefcase had taken on so much water that if he continued trying to swim with it, he would drown or be shot. Finally he had no choice but to let go of the money and swim for his life. In the pitch darkness the battle was pretty much over. The Bahamians had all been killed. One Cuban speed boat and her crew were lost. Millions of dollars of cocaine were destroyed. One of the Stingers was badly damaged, and Mugger was lost.

The Cuban speed boat was able to escape leaving Turk and his crew to assess the damage. The two Stingers turned on their search lights to search the waters for Mugger. The rough ocean and the debris scattered everywhere from the skirmish made it extremely difficult to try to find Mugger. After searching for ten minutes Turk could hear police sirens closing in from the shoreline. Turk blared a fog horn to signal the others and yelled out, "It's time to get the bloody hell out of here before the local authorities detain us." Turk threw the throttle to full power causing the boat to spinout and blast out towards the open sea. As the Stinger was accelerating Saber looked overboard and spotted the money case. Thinking quickly she grabbed a gaff hook and snagged the brief case then flung it aboard. Jawz was in control of the second Stinger and was quick to follow the lead of Turk.

Meanwhile the Bahamian police were firing everything they had from the shoreline at the two Stinger boats. They were convinced that Turk and his crew were drug smugglers. They would soon have their own boats in the water chasing the Stingers. Although Turk was on a beeline for Miami he did make a short stop at one of the outer islands. Turk and Saber went ashore to a small Bahamian orphanage where Turk knew the head sister. Turk knocked on the orphanage door and when the head sister opened the door he gave her a hug. He stepped back a foot and signaled Saber for the briefcase. As he handed it to the sister he said, "Sister Hollis, don't say a word or ask any questions. Take this money and use it quietly and wisely for the kids." The sister gave both Turk and Saber a hug. Turk added, "Thanks for the sentiment, Sister, but we have to get our butts out of here." Turk and Saber ran down the narrow dark streets back towards their boats. The sister stood there in the doorway and bowed her head in prayer thanking God for friends like Turk and Saber and the gift they brought her. Once they were out of sight she yelled, "Lord, protect my friends. They have hearts of gold and mean well."

Meanwhile Benito and his crippled boat headed back to Cuba empty handed. He knew MÁXIMO would probably have him killed. He had nothing. He had lost a million dollars of MÁXIMO's cocaine and a million dollars in US cash. The only thing he had going for him was the fact that MÁXIMO had already killed off most of his lieutenants. Maybe he would keep him around.

As dawn rose on the Florida coast the crew aboard the two Stingers could see the beautiful sight of the glimmering coast, but to their dismay it looked like a fleet of Miami police patrol boats were between them and the shoreline.

Bucko looked at Turk and said," What now, Captain? Do we run, fight, surrender or what?"

Turk smiled and replied, "I think it's an 'or what' proposition." He then pointed up in the air at two Black Hawk choppers dropping down on them. Within two minutes the two crews were aboard and flying away from their police reception, leaving the shot up Stingers for the Miami shore patrol.

CHAPTER 16

Hit and Run

HIT AND RUN

The Black Hawk flew low and fast to stay out of radar tracking. They kept to the coast line so as not to draw attention from anyone inland. All had been quiet for about fifteen minutes, but the silence was broken when a figure stepped out of the co-pilots' seat. The dark figure stepped back to the others. Turk looked up and yelled out, "Storm, what the bloody hell do you want?"

Storm sat down saying, "I want to hear a hell of a good report. So far, all I know is what the Bahamian police department had to say."

Turk snarled back saying, "So let's hear what they bloody said."

Storm replied, "Well, it wasn't a pretty picture." He went on saying, "On the old shipwreck, there were at least ten Bahamians dead bodies strung out all over the ship. Most of them were coated with traces of cocaine dust. Who knows how many millions of dollars of cocaine were destroyed? Next they found a capsized speedboat with dead Cubans in it and floating in the water around the boat. They also said at least three boats fled the scene before their pursuit boats arrived." Storm paused a minute and then asked, "So Turk, tell me; did the Cubans leave the scene of the crime with the money or do you have it?"

Turk jumped up boiling mad. He pointed his finger at Storm's face and yelled, "Now look, mate, we lost one of our good friends last night, and all you can ask is if we stole the bloody money."

Storm jumped to his feet and snapped back at Turk saying, "I never said you stole the money. I asked you if you had the money."

Turk calmed back down and smile. He added, "Yes, Storm, we recovered the money."

Storm looked around and said, "Where the hell is it then?"

Turk replied, "It was spoils of war. They were enemies of the state, and we elected to commandeer their possessions. Being spoils of war collected in the confines of the Bermuda Triangle, the loot is ours."

Storm snapped back, "Well, I've got news for you, buddy boy. When we step ashore you will be stripped of that drug money."

Turk smiled saying, "I think not, mate, since we've already disposed of the booty."

Storm yelled," You what!"

Turk turned to Saber and said, "You tell Agent Storm what happened to the money."

Saber smiled and said, "The poor children of the Bahamas are finally going to get the care they deserve."

"I'll be damned!" yelled Storm. He turned away from the others and made his way back to the cockpit. None of the others could see the smile that covered his face from ear to ear.

Finally the Black Hawks landed back at the base to the surprise of the Phantom's crew. The Phantom was out in the open and tied up at one of the docks. Everything on the Phantom looked brand new. No one would ever have known the damage the Phantom had suffered. As the crew walked around the Phantom admiring her new look, Storm received a call on his cell. The call was short, and Storm seemed unhappy afterwards. Turning to Turk he said, "I've got bad news for you. Before you can head back to Bermuda for a little R and R, we've got a little job for you."

Turk looked surprised, but not upset. He looked over at Storm and asked, "Alright then, what the bloody hell are we going after this time?"

Storm replied, "Our intel has spotted three fast moving boats just inside the Bermuda Triangle tracking northerly."

Turk asked, "Are they Cubans heading to Bermuda?"

Storm replied, "I don't think so. I'd bet money that they are drug smugglers out of Miami. They're trying to skirt around the east coast to avoid the Coast Guard. You can bet New York is their destination."

Turk turned back to the Phantom crew and yelled out, "Mates, it's time to shove off. We've got some Yanks on the run through the Triangle. We've got to stop them before they veer back out of the Triangle. Let's lock and load, and get the hell out of here."

The crew started to scramble. They all knew what needed to be done to get the Phantom ready for a voyage. Within the hour the Phantom was under way and tracking the Miami drug smugglers. Turk knew he would have to catch them before they shifted westerly and left the waters of the Bermuda Triangle.

Within the hour, the Phantom blasted off from the secret base. Turk had the engines wide open. He knew there was very little time to catch up with the smugglers before they left the waters of the Bermuda Triangle.

Turk barked out, "Mulate, let me know as soon as you pick these drug runners up on the radar screen." He turned to Bucko and said, "Here Bucko, take the wheel. The ocean is smooth as glass today so let's show those speed boats who can get down and kick ass."

Bucko took the wheel and replied, "Roger that, Captain. We'll catch up to the drug dealers before they know what hit them."

Turk smiled and added, "That works." He looked over at the rest of the crew and said, "Alright, mates. Let's check our weapons of mass destruction." Turk left the bridge heading for the stern of the ship.

Saber looked at Jawz, Squid, and Dawg and said, "His majesty speaks, I guess we should follow." She turned and left the bridge.

Dawg smiled as he watched Saber leave. He then added, "I like following her."

As they made their way to the stern Turk was already at the Gatling gun firing off a few test rounds towards the horizon. Saber and Squid picked up M16's for backup. Neither of them cared much about firing the big boy's toys. Dawg on the other hand couldn't wait to get his hands on the grenade launcher. Dawg smiled saying, "When we see those bastards, I'm going to blow them sky high."

Saber gave Dawg a disgusted look and said, "Aren't you supposed to ask them to give up first?"

Dawg laughed and replied, "Look sister, that's not my job. I'm trained to shoot first and ask questions later."

Turk looked back at Saber and said, "Not to worry, Saber. It's my job to do the communications here." He then fired off about twenty more rounds with the Gatling gun. Turk added, "There I just sent those bastards a message." All three men laughed while Saber turned her back and walked away.

Several hours later just before dusk Mulate yelled out, "Captain, I picked them up on the radar, but you better come here."

Turk left his post and entered the bridge. Looking at the radar he saw the three blips and asked, "So what's the problem, mate? We've got them in our sights."

Mulate pointed to the screen and said, "See that line across the screen?"

Turk replied, "Yeah, so what?"

Mulate added, "That line is just about the edge of the Bermuda Triangle. Remember we're not to cross it."

Turk snapped back and said, "Look mate, we're out in the middle of nowhere. Who the hell is going to see us if we accidently cross that imaginary line?"

Mulate just shook his head saying, "Mon, you're the Captain." As they closed in on the three boats Mulate noticed another blip off to the northwest. He tapped Turk on the shoulder and said, "Look, we've got company."

Turk looked at the screen and said, "Looking at the size of that blip! It must be a cargo ship on its way to Bermuda."

Mulate added, "We'll have a visual in a few minutes on the three boats."

Turk looked over at Bucko and said, "Remember with three of them they may split and run or turn on us. Be ready to take evasive action."

Bucko replied, "Roger that, Captain".

Turk went back to the Gatling gun and waited. He didn't have to wait very long. The three boats were now within range. Turk yelled out, "Man your stations. I'm going to fire a burst of warning shots over their bows to get their attention." Turk ripped off over fifty shots and then waited for a response. He got a response, but not the one he expected. Men with AK-47's on all three boats fired in rapid succession back at the Phantom causing Bucko to steer in a zig- zag maneuver to avoid being hit.

Turk began firing his Gatling gun non-stop back at the boats. Firing at over a thousand rounds a minute, his bullets were shredding the back sides of the speed boats. Turk turned back to Dawg and yelled out, "Fire a couple of those grenades into the middle boat."

Dawg didn't need to be told twice. He was ready for action. In seconds Dawg jumped up, took aim and fired both grenades. Both grenades scored direct hits on the middle boat. When the smoke settled there was no trace of the middle speed boat. There was only floating debris in the water.

Turk signaled Bucko to close in for the kill; but before he could, Mulate grabbed his arm saying, "Look mate, that big blip was not a small cargo ship. It's a US Coast Guard cutter."

Bucko said, "So what. They'll help us." Before another word could be said The Coast Guard cutter began firing everything in their arsenal at all three boats including the Phantom.

Turk started yelling at the Coast Guard cutter to stop firing, but to no avail. Turk knew he couldn't return fire. He left the Gatling gun and signaled the others to follow him to the bridge. The entire crew found themselves on the floor of the bridge avoiding bullets ripping through the bridge. Turk looked over at Mulate and said, "Why the hell are they shooting at us?"

Mulate snapped back, "I think it's simple. It's almost dark. They're looking for three speed boats and guess what they found: three, all firing bullets at them."

Turk replied, "Yeah, but don't you think they've heard of us by now?"

Mulate added, "Maybe so, but did you forget? We're not exactly in the Bermuda Triangle anymore."

With a sick look on his face, Turk said, "Oh crap!" He looked over at Bucko and yelled, "Throw the Phantom in stealth mode and get us the hell out of here before they blow us out of the water."

The Phantom turned sharply to starboard and with no engine sounds left the dark night air without a trace.

Meanwhile from the bridge on the Coast Guard cutter the first officer called to the captain, "Captain, we've captured two of the drug smugglers' speed boats, but one of them is missing."

The captain looked at the radar and said, "Are you sure we didn't sink it? There's no sign of it on the radar."

The first mate replied, "There's lots of debris out there, but that was a huge speed boat. It must have got away, sir."

The captain replied, "Secure these drug smugglers, and I'll call in for some chopper support with night vision. We'll find those bastards. They won't get away.

Meanwhile back on the Phantom, Turk and the others were making sure no one was hurt. Turk looked at the radar screen and said, "Bucko, my mate, I do believe we're now out of their radar tracking range. Let's get the hell out of here and go home to Bermuda."

Bucko and the rest of the crew smiled. They were all ready for a little R&R. Bucko shut down the stealth mode and electric turbines. A second later the main engines were fired up and the Phantom was running at seventy knots towards home. Tomorrow they could lick their wounds and rest.

CHAPTER 17

Wanted Dead or Deader

WANTED
DEAD OR DEADER

It was another beautiful day in Guantánamo Bay, but the drug lord MÁXIMO and his lieutenants Bento and Gitmo had failed to appreciate that fact. MÁXIMO was just about at his wits end. Half of his lieutenants were dead. He had lost millions of dollars over the last few months, and he feared the Columbian drug lords might try to destroy his operation. He must crush the Bermuda vigilantes so his drug empire could return to normal.

MÁXIMO and his lieutenants were inspecting one of the main drug processing centers in his massive compound. He began screaming, ranting and raving at anyone or anything that moved. He was struggling to find a solution to his problems. Finally, he yelled out, "I've got it, amigos! We'll send an assassination team to Bermuda to kill these vigilantes."

Benito with a surprised look on his face said, "Forgive me, lord, but Cubans in Bermuda will stand out like a sore thumb. Plus if the Americans find out they'll try to intercept us."

MÁXIMO disgustedly snapped back, "I know that, you idiot! We'll send our death squad to Portugal first. I'll have Portuguese passports waiting for them there. From Portugal, they'll visit Bermuda as tourists. No one will be the wiser."

Gitmo asked, "How are we going to get them the proper weapons in Bermuda?"

MÁXIMO replied, "That may have been a problem a long time ago, but with all the shootings going on in Bermuda, believe me, we'll find plenty of hand guns there."

Gitmo asked, "Will that be enough firepower? I hear their ghost ship is loaded with state-of-the-art weaponry."

MÁXIMO smiled and added, "Well amigo, these vigilantes think they're clever. We'll be like a black wind and be on the top of them before they know what happened. We'll catch them one at a time, and in less than a week they'll all be dead. If that doesn't work we'll kidnap one of them as a hostage and force the others out in the open."

Gitmo smiled and asked, "Who do we have to lead these paid assassins and where can we find such professionals?"

MÁXIMO turned to Gitmo with a smile and said, "My little brother, it is you who will lead our small band of night fighters."

With another surprised look on this face, Gitmo said, "I thought these men were assassins. Now you call them night fighters. So who the hell are they?"

MÁXIMO replied, "Well, actually, my friends in the Cuba military are going to loan me a squad of jungle fighters. "

Gitmo asked, "What if one gets killed or captured in Bermuda? How's the Cuban government going to explain that?"

MÁXIMO added, "Not a problem. These men have no identities, no prints, no dental records anywhere. They will never be traced to Cuba. They'll be strictly Portugal nationals with fake IDs." Now, my friend, you'd better go get ready for tomorrow. You're on a flight to Portugal to meet up with your friends."

The two men shook hands, and Gitmo headed back to his quarters to pack.

CHAPTER 18

Igor the Terrible

IGOR THE TERRIBLE

The Phantom was making remarkable time on her way back home to Bermuda. Most of the crew members were in their bunks relaxing, enjoying the voyage home, without worrying about any surprise attacks from drug smugglers or bounty hunters. Turk was sipping on a cold brew in his captain's chair on the bridge while Bucko was piloting the Phantom home. Mulate was keeping tabs on the ship's instruments and navigational devices plus keeping Bucko company. The Phantom always traveled under radio silence making sure no other ship or tracking instruments could pick the ship up. The downside was that most of the time the crew on the Phantom were unaware of current events around the world.

As the Phantom closed in within two hundred miles of Bermuda, Bucko broke the silence by saying, "Mulate, since you're just sitting there and doing nothing, get off your butt, turn the radar system on and check if there's any surprises between us and Bermuda."

Mulate slowly got up out of his chair and walked over to the ship's radar screen. After staring at the screen for a minute he yelled out, "What the hell!"

Turk jumped up out of his chair and raced over to the radar screen. Turk turned to Bucko and said, "Bucko, get your butt over here and look at this. It's the biggest bloody storm I've ever seen. It must cover half the Atlantic Ocean."

Although it was hurricane season in the Atlantic Ocean over ninety percent of the hurricanes never come close to Bermuda. They would either swerve to the west and threaten the Caribbean, or go north and simply miss Bermuda. After all, Bermuda only occupies twenty-one square miles in millions of square miles of the Atlantic Ocean. This hurricane was different. It was on a direct course for Bermuda.

Bucko looked at the screen and said, "We're not heading into that storm are we, captain?"

Turk snapped back, "With the speed of the Phantom we'll be back in Bermuda and locked down before the bloody storm hits." He looked at Mulate and added, "Mulate, get the Bermuda Weather Service on the radio and find out what we're facing for sure."

Mulate replied , "Roger that, captain." He turned and picked up his headset and contacted Bermuda. A few minutes later Mulate laid his headset down and said, "Well mates, its one bad ass hurricane on a collision course for Bermuda. Harbor Radio is turning all ships away from Bermuda unless their arrival is imminent. We're only hours away, but the outer bands of the hurricane have already hit Bermuda. That means in a couple of hours Igor will have us in his grips. "

Turk interrupted Mulate saying, "Well, that's not a problem for us. They'll never know we entered Bermuda waters."

Mulate continued on, "Mon, Hurricane Igor right now is a category two hurricane with winds of over one hundred miles per hour."

Bucko chimed in saying, "That's not so bad, mate."

Mulate snapped back, "I forgot to mention the damn hurricane is over six hundred miles wide. A hurricane like that is going to take over thirty hours to pass over Bermuda. Can you imagine the kind of damage it's going to do?"

Turk added, "Thanks for the report. Go let the rest of the crew know it's all hands on deck and to be prepared for a rough ride home." Mulate left the bridge. Turk turned to Bucko saying, "Well, old buddy, we're about to find out how seaworthy the Phantom is. Set a direct course for Bermuda and be prepared to hit some thirty to forty foot waves between us and Bermuda."

Bucko walked back over to the ship's wheel and said, "We're racing straight into the Bermuda Triangle and the eye of Hurricane Igor. That can't be a sensible combination, mate."

Turk gave Bucko a pat on the back and said, "We've been through worse than this." Turk turned away and walked over to the ship map table. As he stared at the map he thought to himself, "We're in for one hell of a ride tonight."

Meanwhile the rest of the crew had made their way to their assigned stations. Jawz and Squid were in the engine room waiting to deal with any possible mechanical problems. Saber took her place in the infirmary in case there were any injuries. Dawg roamed the ship ready to assist wherever needed. Now all they could do was wait as darkness fell. It was going to be a long night. As every hour passed the winds and waves kept picking up. It wasn't long before the Phantom was in the middle of the full blown storm. The Phantom's crew was being thrown from one side of the ship to the other as each crushing wave pounded down on her. Turk was beginning to think that maybe they should have made a run for it in the opposite direction.

About an hour out of Bermuda with the ocean conditions about at their worse, Mulate yelled out, "Captain! I've picked up a small vessel to our west about twenty miles. I've been watching it for about the last five minutes, and they appear to be out of control."

Turk quickly came over to the radar screen to see. He asked, "I wonder if it's floundering because it's abandoned?"

The conversation was being broadcast through the entire ship's sound system. A second later Saber spoke up, "For God sakes, Turk, we can't go without checking on that boat. They'll never survive the hurricane."

Turk yelled back, "Saber, can it! There's no way in hell I'm going to leave that boat out there in the open seas in trouble."

Saber replied back in a much lower tone, "You're a good man, captain. Thank you."

Turk turned back to Bucko and said, "Bucko, change our course to due west and let's find that boat." He then said to Mulate, "See if you can make radio contact with them." Both men got to work with their assignments.

After ten minutes of trying to raise radio contact with the boat Mulate looked at Turk and said, "No reply from the boat. Do you want me to keep trying?"

Turk replied, "Don't stop until we have a visual." He grabbed the ship's mike and said, "All hands to the bridge except for Squid. You stay with the engines. The rest of you bring grappling hooks, ropes and life preservers." Within in minutes the crew was on the bridge ready to attempt a rescue. Turk walked over to the control panel and flipped the switches for the search lights. He said, "Based on the radar we're almost right on top of them now. With the waves being over thirty feet high it was almost impossible to locate anything by line of vision.

Out of nowhere at the top of a wave crest Dawg yelled out, "Ship twelve o'clock high on the bottom side of this wave."

Turk screamed out, "Bucko! Reverse engines full or we'll crush that boat!"

Bucko slammed the engines in reverse, but it was too late. The Phantom crashed down on the sailboat catching its bow. The sail boat flipped one hundred eighty degrees and impaled itself on the front Gatling gun of the Phantom.

Turk yelled, "Everyone except Bucko and Mulate follow me. We've got to get to the sailboat before it breaks apart and is washed off the deck." With ropes tied to each other Turk, Dawg, Saber and Jawz left the bridge and made their way one behind the other towards the wrecked sailboat. Between the high winds and the ship rocking it was almost impossible to keep ones balance. After making it to the sailboat Turk signaled Dawg to follow him aboard the sailboat while Saber and Jawz waited outside. Once on the sailboat Turk signaled Dawg to check the deck out while he went below deck. Turk looked around below deck, but all he could see was a huge pile of debris in the bow of the sailboat. Turk quickly started digging through the debris looking for a sign of life and to his amazement he saw something moving behind some water soaked blankets. Turk reached through the blankets and felt something wiggling in his hands. Turk got a little nervous and yelled out for Dawg, "Get your bloody butt down here, Dawg! I need your help."

Dawg tripped down the steps, and as the sailboat rocked he fell in the middle of the debris. As he lifted up his head he felt a big tongue licking his face. Turk yelled out, "Well, I'll be damned! Dawg just found a dog."

Turk looked down and smiled saying, "It's a bloody Great Dane." This had to be the largest dog Turk had ever seen. The Great Dane was dark gray with small black spots dotted all over his body. There was also one large black spot that completely encircled his right eye. He must have weighed over two hundred pounds. The sailboat took a sudden shift and knocked Dawg and Turk off their feet.

Back on the deck Saber screamed, "You better get the hell out of there fast! The sailboat is just about ready to break up into pieces and slide off the deck."

Turk grabbed the collar of the Great Dane and pulled him up the stairs. As they made their way back to the topside Jawz yelled up, "Any luck with survivors?"

Turk yelled back, "Yeah, we found one." Then they jumped off the sailboat.

Just then a monster wave swept over the deck knocking the sailboat off the Phantom and back into the rough seas.

As everyone regained his sea legs Turk looked around and yelled out, "Where's Saber?"

Dawg pointed overboard and yelled, "There she is—in the water!" But before anyone could throw her a life preserver, the Great Dane jumped overboard and swam directly towards her. The large dog got to her in less than a minute. Saber grabbed his collar as the massive dog began swimming back towards the Phantom. When the dog and Saber came alongside the ship Turk, Dawg and Jawz reached into the water and pulled the two on deck.

Once back inside the bridge Turk wrapped Saber in a blanket while Dawg and Jawz tried their best to dry off the monster dog. Dawg yelled at Jawz, "Hell, man, can't you hold that dog still? He won't stop licking me. I'm getting wetter than he is."

Saber laughed and said, "From one Dawg to another dog, he's just showing his gratitude for saving his life."

Dawg replied, "Well, I wish he would be a little less grateful."

Jawz asked, "What do you think happened to everyone else onboard?"

Turk joined in on the conversation saying, "They must have been washed overboard when the bloody storm hit. I'm guessing the dog was locked below deck; that's the only reason he survived."

As Dawg finished drying the dog and himself he asked, "Turk, when we get back to Bermuda what are you going to do with this shipwreck survivor?"

Saber answered first, "I'm sure our captain will throw him a bone and just let him go."

With a frown on his face, Turk snapped back, "What in the bloody hell do you think I am, Saber? I'm not that coldblooded. This big pooch didn't hesitate to put his own life at risk and save your butt."

Saber's face had now turned red from embarrassment. She just sat there and gave the Great Dame a hug.

Turk went on to say, "Look, mates, I think this bloody dog should become our ship's mascot. He appears to be the best lifesaver onboard."

Saber added, "Well if we're going to keep him, what are we going to call the big boy?"

Jawz replied, "With all the spots we could call him Spot. Or maybe since he has an eye patch like you, Turk, we could give him a pirate's name or call him Patch."

Turk smiled and said, "I know just what we'll call him. It's simple. We'll call him Igor. We found him in the middle of Hurricane Igor, and he's as big as a monster so the name fits. Igor it is." Turk stood up and added, "Let's all get back to our stations. This hurricane's only going to get worse. Saber, you can keep Igor company for awhile until he settles down."

The rest of the crew went back to work. Saber sat there for awhile with Igor laying his head in her lap. She looked down at the mammoth dog and said, "Igor fella, you've got to be the biggest lap dog in the world. But you know what? That's fine with me. You rest now because you're going to have one hell of a time keeping that new master of yours, Turk, out of trouble. Neither one of us want to see that big baboon hurt himself." Saber stroked Igor's back for a few minutes and quietly stood up and left the bridge to return to her duties. Igor just laid there relaxing as if he knew he was in safe hands.

The Phantom was now within ten miles of Bermuda and they were going to arrive at the height of the storm. If the Phantom could survive the last ten miles of hell it would have to pass through, she could withstand anything. Turk and Bucko were now locked in the bridge for the duration of the voyage. Igor showed no fear. He got up from his nap and made his way over to the bridge's front window and stood there looking out the window at the monster storm. Bucko looked over at Turk and said, "Captain, I think we've acquired a fearless mate on this voyage." Both men laughed for a few seconds; then Turk turned to the ships wheel while Bucko managed the instrument panels. The Phantom was now bouncing almost out of control from killer waves that were bashing her from all directions. Turk kept trying to steer the Phantom into the massive waves, but every time he tried, the violent wind and waves pushed the Phantom in another direction.

Bucko looked over at Turk and said, "Captain, we're only about five miles out now. Do you think we're going to make it in this monster hurricane?"

Turk yelled back, "Hell yes, we're going to make it, mate." He looked over at Igor and yelled, "Igor, old boy, don't you think we can make it?" Igor jumped up on his back legs and with his front paws on the bridge window. He was now taller than Turk. He looked over at Turk and let out the most earth shattering howling. He must have howled for five minutes solid. He suddenly stopped and sat back down. Turk looked over at Bucko and said, "Well, there you have it, mate. Igor says we're going to make it."

Bucko replied, "Well, I hope he knows his business." No sooner had Bucko stopped talking when a fifty foot wave came crashing on the starboard side of the Phantom almost flipping the ship onto her side.

Turk screamed out, "Full power!" and the Phantom blasted her way through the rogue wave.

Bucko got on the ship's intercom and yelled out, "All crew report in. Is everyone alright?" It took awhile, but everyone finally answered and all were accounted for. They were now within a mile of Bermuda and Bucko asked, 'Captain, are we just going to try to make it to St. George's Harbour?"

Turk replied, "Sorry, mate, we've got to bear this storm out a little longer and make it to the Great Sound and onto Morgan's Point." Bucko was tired and only wanted this voyage to be over. All be could muster was, "Crap". Turk tried to cheer him up by saying, "Come on, mate. Once we get into our safe haven we'll sleep for a couple of days, and then hit all the pubs on Front Street."

Bucko gave Turk a salute saying , "Aye, Captain." The two laughed and Igor let out a loud bark in agreement.

The Phantom finally made it into Bermuda waters and slowly made her way along the North Shore. The worst of the hurricane had now veered slightly to the west making the effects of the storm somewhat less threatening. It was now in the early morning hours, but still very dark and overcast. The winds were still pushing eighty miles per hour making it very dangerous as the ship slowly cruised through the Great Sound heading for Morgan's Point. Because there was not a soul out on the island this morning, Turk never bothered to switch the system over to stealth mode.

Little did Turk know that he was being watched by a pair of binoculars from the top of Gibbs Hill Lighthouse in South Hampton. It was not the lighthouse night watchman. The watchman had been pushed down the circular stairs and fallen to his death. He was lying in a pool of blood. The Bermuda police would believe his fall had been an accident. The perpetrators of this evil deed were three of the Cuban night fighters sent by MÁXIMO. One of the Cubans continued to watch the Phantom as it motored into the Sound. As the Phantom passed by the lighthouse, the Cuban lost sight of her in the stormy weather. He threw down the binoculars and began cussing in Spanish. Finally he calmed down and yelled out, "Those marauders just vanished into the storm."

One of the other Cubans interrupted him saying, "Not to worry, amigo. We now know the Phantom is back in Bermuda. They have to be in hiding somewhere close by. We'll simply stake out the surrounding area and wait for a break."

The first Cuban replied, "You're right, my brother. Time is on our side. We'll wait, watch and then butcher them when the moment is right." The three Cubans made their way out of the light house with the decision to begin tracking the Phantom and her crew tomorrow.

Meanwhile the Phantom made her way into the hidden cove at Morgan's Point. Slowly they entered into the secret cave where the massive concrete doors concealed them from the outside world. They would have time to make the long overdue needed repairs to the Phantom. Turk would give his crew a day of rest, but they would have to stay inside the cave with the Phantom. There would be no visits to the outside world just yet. After the Phantom was back to one hundred percent, and only then would they get a night out on the town.

CHAPTER 19

The Stake Out

THE STAKE OUT

The repairs to the Phantom went very quickly. The high winds from Hurricane Igor went pretty much unnoticed in the underground air tight chamber the Phantom was docked in. Not to mention that the entire crew was slightly distracted by their new crew member. Igor the Great Dane was actually a young dog in spite of its massive size. He thought the entire crew of the Phantom were his playmates. There wasn't a tool onboard that Igor didn't think was a chew toy.

It was late in the afternoon when Turk, Bucko, and Mulate entered the ship's bridge to review the progress on the repairs. As they walked over to the map table Turk yelled out, "What the hell is that slop all over the maps?"

Mulate laughed and said, "Captain, that's slobber from our new crew member."

Bucko joined in the fun adding, "Yep, I think we have a new navigator who's going to give Mulate a run for his money." He then looked under the map table and continued, "Igor is still hard at it, sir. It looks like he's eating one of our maps for a late afternoon snack."

Turk was now very annoyed. He stomped over to the bridge mike and yelled out, "Saber, to the bridge and pronto."

A few minutes later Saber made her way to the bridge. As she stepped through the hatch she asked, "Yes Captain, what is it?"

Still looking over a map, Turk pointed down below the table and said, "I believe Igor could use a walk on some dry land. I don't think my maps can stand much more of his scrutiny."

The hurricane had now passed, and Saber was also ready to step foot on some dry stable land. She let out a short whistle and said, "Come on, boy. Let's leave these old stuffy guys alone." Igor jumped up with a mouth full of rolled up maps in his mouth and ran over to Saber. Saber laughed at the sight, but since no one else on the bridge laughed she took the maps out of Igor's mouth and said, "I think we better leave these for the Captain."

She handed the soggy maps to Turk and left the bridge with Igor. Once outside Saber was amazed how clear the skies were. One would never have known a hurricane had just passed through Bermuda except for the fact that there was extensive damage to the trees and greenery. Since Morgan's Point was sealed off from the public, Saber and Igor had a very large area to walk in without being noticed by anyone. At least that's what Saber thought. She had failed to notice that in some undergrowth closeby someone was indeed watching her every movement. As she walked closer to the undergrowth area Igor began to get restless. His muzzle went high in the air taking in the scent of something sinister. All of a sudden Igor began growling and lunged so hard at the overgrowth area the leash snapped in two leaving Saber a piece of leather, but no dog.

Saber yelled out, "Igor, come back here!" But before she could say anything else a frantic commotion erupted in the bushes. All she could hear was Igor growling and barking and several male voices screaming out in Spanish. The three Cuban tumbled out of the overgrowth waving pistols in the air.

One of the Cubans raised his pistol and pointed it at Saber. He yelled out, "Pretty one, call your dog off!" Before Saber could say anything Igor

146

turned and jumped on the Cuban knocking him down. Igor stood over him with his paws on his chest.

Another Cuban turned and pointed his pistol at Igor. Saber saw him and screamed out, "Don't shoot him!". But it was too late; the Cuban fired off a round from his pistol. Igor let out a growl and turned to charge the other Cuban, but before he ran three feet his front legs collapsed. Igor hit the ground like a ton of bricks. His body was now motionless. Saber screamed out, "You murderers!"

The Cuban who had shot Igor laughed at Saber and said, "Shut up, woman." He fired a shot at her striking her in the chest. The shot was at such close range it caused Saber to fly backwards striking a tree as she crumpled to the ground. The third Cuban, Gitmo, wrote out a quick note and slipped it under Igor's collar. He then looked at his comrades saying, "Amigos, grab the girl and get her to the boat before the others show up." One of the two Cubans picked up Saber and threw her over his shoulder. Another one ran ahead to the waiting boat while Gitmo followed close behind making sure no one would be following them. Once reaching the boat the Cuban carrying Saber dumped her lifeless body on a bench in the boat. Within minutes they were speeding away from Morgan's Point. They were on a direct course for a small yacht anchored just outside the Great Sound. Gitmo had decided that kidnapping one of the crew would be far easier than trying to kill the entire crew in Bermuda. He knew MÁXIMO would prefer to have them in Cuba where he could personally witness their deaths.

Meanwhile back on the bridge Turk turned his head in the direction of the shots yelling, "Those were gunshots, mates. Where in the hell did they come from?"

Turk wasn't waiting to try to figure it out. He spun out of his chair, and as he ran out of the bridge's hatch he reached up and grabbed an M16 that was racked above the door. He never looked back to see if Mulate and Bucko were following. Neither Bucko nor Mulate needed an invitation; they were just steps behind Turk. As Turk shoved the concealed door opening to the surface he could see something laying down just off the road in some bushes. Turk signaled the other two to split off in different directions to surround the body. Turk was worried Saber had been in an accident or even shot. As he grew closer he was relieved that the body was not Saber, but to his shock it was Igor. Turk dropped to his knees picking up Igor's lifeless head and yelled out, "What bloody bastards! Who would kill a dog and kidnap Saber? When I catch up with them they're all dead men."

Just then to the shock of all three men Igor began to move his big lanky body. Mulate looked down at Igor and said," Wait a minute, mon. This dog was shot with a tranquilizer gun. The big boy is going to be okay."

Bucko reached down to his collar and said, "Look, here's a note of some type." He opened it up and read it. After a few seconds he handed the note to Turk who could see the worried look on his face.

Turk read the note then wadded it up in his hand crushing it. He yelled out, "Those bloody Cuban bastards have taken her for ransom."

Mulate asked, "What the hell do they want her for?"

Bucko replied, "They want us and the Phantom, mate."

With a swift kick in the gravel, Turk stood up saying, "One thing for sure, they're going to get us, but not in the way they expected to." He turned to the other two and added, "Get back to the ship and round up the crew. Let them know we're going on a hunting trip for a pack of wolves. We'll catch those bastards long before they get to Cuba." The others did what they were told while Turk began going through his countdown list to take the boat out to the open ocean.

CHAPTER 20

The Race is on

THE RACE IS ON

Within hours the Phantom was cruising out of the Great Sound under the cover of darkness in stealth mode. Turk knew that even though the Cubans had a half day lead on the Phantom they would eventually catch up to the Stinger speed boats. Once clear of the Great Sound Turk clicked on the mike to the ship's radio and said, "All stations report their status now." Within minutes all stations replied with the green light go signal. Turk replied back with the mike, "Mulate, plot your course for Cuba, but be ready to intercept those bloody bastards."

Mulate responded, "You got it, mon. All systems are set; let's go kick some Cuban butts."

Turk turned to look at Bucko. Bucko responded with his arm stretched straight up giving Turk 'a thumbs up'. Turk smiled and shut down the stealth electric turbines. He next fired up the diesel engines and yelled out, "Give me everything you've got, Scotty!" He threw the throttle forward to the one hundred percent setting. The Phantom lunged for a split second. The engines roared sending the ship across the ocean like a guided missile. With only a few hours head start Turk felt he could catch up with the Stingers in twenty four hours.

Even at the high speeds the Phantom was traveling, the next twenty four hours seemed like an eternity for Turk and the crew. They were worried about how Saber was being held captive. Turk had the entire crew on the bridge for a short briefing. Bucko, Jawz, Squid, Dawg, and Mulate were all present and, of course, Igor. Turk looked at the crew and said, "Alright mates, soon we'll catch up with those bastards who have Saber. I know we all want to blast their asses from here to Cuba and back, but we have to save Saber first."

Dawg yelled out, "Right on, brother. Then we'll blow them to hell."

The men were all on edge, and Turk sensed it. He looked at the crew once more and said, "Bucko, you and Igor stay on the bridge with me. We may have to pull some slick maneuvers to outwit these drug runners." He then turned to the others and added, "Dawg, station yourself at the Gatling gun. Mulate, you stay close to the rocket launcher, but don't get an itchy trigger finger. In fact that goes for all of you, we don't have a clue where on the boat Saber is being held. Jawz, you and Squid use those M16's over there on the wall, and each of you keep a grappling hook. We'll board them when we come along side. Any questions?"

The bridge went quiet and without saying another word, they left the bridge going to their respective stations. The wait was not long. A couple of hours later, just about dusk, Bucko nudged Turk on the shoulder saying, "Look Captain, a blip just popped up on the screen, and it's moving almost as fast as we are."

Turk smiled, "Well mate, as long as they're just moving almost as fast as us, we're in good shape."

Bucko snapped back, "Wait a minute, Captain. There's the blip on the screen split into two blips, and they're now running side by side. What do you make of that?"

Turk replied, "Those drug smugglers must have radar and can see us coming."

Bucko asked, "Should we switch to stealth mode, Captain?"

Turk shook his head saying, "No, if we go to stealth mode now we'll have to slow down, and we'll never catch up to them. They now know we're coming, and they'll be ready for us. Since they have two Stingers our job just got more dangerous. It may be impossible for us to know which Stinger has Saber on board." With that he slammed his fist down on the red battle stations button which set off the ship's warning sirens all over the Phantom. Igor began howling, and Bucko didn't know which sound was worse— the blaring sirens or Igor's howling.

The two Stingers were now in visual sight of the Phantom. Turk could see that they were both peeling off in opposite direction in hopes to lure the Phantom into a trap or to force the Phantom to follow only one of the Stingers. Turk looked over at Bucko and said, "These bloody bastards are smart, but not that smart." He yelled out to Dawg, " As fast as you can Dawg, fire at the bows of each of the Stingers. Do it before they turn; maybe we can knock out their engines."

Dawg didn't even bother with a reply to Turk. He took aim at the Stinger on the left and ripped off a thousand rounds at it. Without waiting for the smoke to clear and check for damage, he swung around and opened fire on the next Stinger with a deadly barrage of lethal bullets.

Finally when the smoke cleared the Stinger on the left was listing in the water and appeared to be sinking. Although the Stinger on the right had bullet damage across her bow, it seemed intact.

Just as Turk was about to take on the undamaged Stinger an explosion ripped through the bow of the Phantom. When the smoke cleared Squid yelled out, "Captain, take evasive action at 10 o'clock high. A chopper with mini rockets has their sights set on us."

Turk was caught with his pants down. All he could do was to break off the engagement and take evasive action just to survive. The Phantom fired off heat seeping debris in hopes to attract rocket fire. Next he plotted a zigzag course for the Phantom to follow hoping to confuse the rocket fire. To the surprise of the crew of the Phantom the chopper turned back and flew over to the disabled Stinger. Once hovering over the Stinger, a rescue bucket was lowered. A few seconds later Turk could see someone pushing Saber into the basket. A minute later the basket and Saber were in the chopper. The chopper turned back to the Phantom and fired another rocket directly at her.

Turk screamed out, "Mulate, intercept that rocket before it blows us out of the water!" Mulate spun the turret around and fired off a rocket. The two rockets collided within fifty yards of the Phantom. The dual explosion knocked the entire crew to the deck.

As the crew slowly recovered from the explosion, Jawz began firing his M16 at the disabled Stinger. Turk yelled out, "Forget that Stinger! It's the other one we have to watch now".

Bucko interrupted by saying, "Captain, I think you got it wrong. Look again at that Stinger." Bucko was right. The crew had abandoned the Stinger, and the ship was on auto pilot for a collision course with the Phantom. At the same time Gitmo was at the wheel of the other Stinger, and he had it at full speed on a direct course for the Phantom from the opposite direction. The Phantom was now squarely in between the two stingers and under heavy fire. Turk yelled out, "Mulate, take out the disabled Stinger with a few rockets". He turned to Dawg and yelled, "Unload that Gatling gun on the other Stinger, and hold on to your butts." With the firing from all directions and explosions no one could see anything. Turk waited as long as he could, being blinded from all the smoke. He looked over at Igor and said, "Is it a go, old boy?" Igor replied with a huge bark. Bucko just stood there with a dumb look on his face. Turk threw the throttle wide open and just as the Phantom blasted from its position, the two Stingers crashed head on to each other creating an explosion that could be seen for miles. As soon as they had cleared to a safe area, Turk stopped the Phantom to view the skirmish area. Both Stingers were melted together as if they were one ship. They were burning out of control with floating flaming wreckage parts totally circling the boats. MÁXIMO had just lost another lieutenant along with two more boats.

Bucko spoke up saying, "Captain, should we swing around and check for survivors?"

Turk snapped back, "Hell no! We're not in the rescue business, and I'm damn sure we're not taking these killers prisoners. These bloody drug smugglers are nothing but shark bait. They will get what they deserve. May they bloody well rot in Hell."

Turk paused for a minute to collect himself; then all of a sudden it hit him. Where in the hell was the chopper and Saber? Turk yelled out, "Did any of you see what happened to the chopper?"

Squid spoke up, "Captain, while the battle was going on I thought for sure I saw the chopper flying off in a southerly direction."

Turk was pissed. He kicked the door on the bridge and said, "Now those bastards have us just where they want us. The advantage will be theirs. Now we have to deal with them on their home turf in Cuba." When Turk looked around to the others for a comment, he noticed something else. He screamed out, "Where in the hell is Jawz?"

They each walked over to where Jawz had been stationed at the start of the fight, but there was no trace of him except for blood spattered all over the deck. His M16 and grappling hook were also missing. His friends looked for him for the next twenty minutes. There was no sign of his body in the water. Turk had already come to the realization that he had just lost another good friend.

Turk gathered the remaining crew together at the bow of the ship. After saying a brief prayer for Jawz, Turk went on to say, "We're sailing into a trap that we may not survive. We've got a damaged ship that somehow we have to repair on the open sea, and to make matters worse, we probably don't have enough crew to run this ship. You all know what needs to be done, so let's get at it. The crew dispersed. They all knew that at most they had only a few days to get the Phantom back to battle worthiness.

CHAPTER 21

The Storm at Sea

THE STORM AT SEA

The next two days the crew worked almost around the clock trying to get the Phantom battle worthy. Turk knew if the crew didn't finish the repairs soon they would be too exhausted to fight.

Later that day Turk called the crew to the bridge for a progress report. The reports had gone well so far. Turk looked at Squid and said, "Well, Squid, have you been saving the best for last?"

Squid looked down at the deck for a few moments then looked back at Turk saying, "No, my report is not a good one, Turk."

Impatiently Turk said, "Well, just give it to me down and dirty, mate."

Squid replied, "Alright then. Working on the ship's engines is not my job, but shorthanded as we are someone had to do it."

Turk nodded in agreement and said, "I know that. Please continue with the bloody report."

Trying to choose his works carefully, Squid went on to say, "The diesel engines are fine, but the battery turbines took a hit from the Stingers. They are working, but they may not be reliable when we need them."

Turk replied, "Mates, with or without turbines, the Phantom is going to rescue Saber and destroy the lair of this drug lord. I'm going to give each of you an out with no strings attached." Turk paused for a moment then continued, "Soon we will be passing Turks Island. If any of you want out I'll put you on a life raft a mile out. The currents will carry you directly to the island. From there you can find your own way home, or if we survive we'll pick you up on the way back to Bermuda."

Dawg pulled out his knife and slammed it down on the table. The blade imbedded itself an inch into the table. Not a word was said, but one after another Bucko, Squid and Mulate imbedded their knives one after another on the table. Turk knew this meant that his crew would go down with the ship if need be. One after another Turk went to each man and gave each of them a bear hug.

Before Turk could say anything else, Bucko interrupted the moment by saying, "Look, Captain, at the radar screen. We've got a good size vessel on a direct course for us."

Turk looked at the screen and said, "It's coming at us from the west as the crow flies. It must be an American ship of some type." Turk turned to the others saying, "Mates, just in case there some bad asses, man your battle stations." The crew ran out of the bridge to man their stations. Turk decided to play a wait and see game. He knew he could outrun any ship on the ocean, and they still had the weapons to protect themselves. They did not have to wait long. About ten minutes later Turk could see the distinct red bands on the ship. He knew it was a United States Coast Guard vessel. He only wondered why they were so far out to sea.

Through the ship's broadcast system Turk shouted, "Men, stand down. It's a friendly."

Bucko walked over to Turk and asked, "That ship is still so far away, how can you tell it's a friendly? And who the hell is it anyway?"

Turk smiled and replied, "See those red bands on the ship?"

Bucko nodded his head. Turk went on to say, "Those are the markings of a Coast Guard ship. I know we never see one because we're always trying to avoid them." Turk added, "Stop the engines. Let them approach us."

A few more minutes passed before the Coast Guard ship was within fifty yards of the Phantom. A small boat was lowered to the ocean with four men onboard. Turk could see three were Coast Guard officers and one must have been a civilian. He was dressed in a casual tropical shirt. As the boat approached the Phantom Turk could not believe his eyes. He yelled out, "Storm, you bloody bastard, what the hell are you doing here?"

The boat pulled alongside of the Phantom. One of the officers onboard the boat threw Squid a rope to tie the two boats together. After that was done, Storm yelled out, "Permission to come aboard, Captain."

Turk yelled back, "You ass! Get your butt on onboard." The four men came aboard and after a brief introduction Turk asked, "What the hell do you want Storm, and how the hell did you track us down?"

Storm smiled and replied, "Don't forget, brother, my country built this ship. Whenever there is an interest the Phantom can be tracked, even in stealth mode, by my agency. Having said that, most of the time we don't care to know where you are or what you are doing."

This was news to Turk and it was an understatement to say he was a bit disturbed by what Storm had just told him. Before Turk could say anything Storm added, "Turk, get over it. Yes, big brother might watch you occasionally, but that's the way it is."

Turk snapped back, "Alright then, but is there anything else I should know?" He paused for a moment waiting for a response from Storm that never came. Turk went on to say, "Well then, what the hell are you tracking us down for right now?"

Storm replied, "A couple of days ago on satellite we could tell you had a nasty run in with some drug smugglers. We also know that the Phantom took some pretty good hits. We saw a chopper at the site for a brief period, and then it was gone. What was that all about?"

Turk pulled out a paper from his pocket and handed it to Storm. He then said, "The bloody bastards kidnapped Saber and took her to that GPS location. We're on our way to get her."

After seeing the GPS location Storm said, "Wait just a damn minute. Do you know where you're going?"

Turk replied, "Hell yes, I know it's Cuba, but this bloody drug lord has Saber. We're going to get her back and take down this bastard at the same time."

Storm shook his head in disagreement and said, "Are you serious? This is a concealed cove right next door to Guantanamo Bay Naval Base. This drug lord is the largest Caribbean drug lord, and he has the protection of the Cuban government. He's taunted us for years, but we can't stop him."

Turk added, "Well mate, then it's up to us to go in and kick his ass."

Storm replied, "I think not, my friend. MÁXIMO would like nothing better than for you to come cruising into his small fortress and create an international incident."

Turk interrupted by saying, "We'll put this MÁXIMO out of business before he knows what hit him."

Storm added, "That sounds good except you're forgetting a small detail."

Turk snapped back, "What the bloody hell is that?"

Storm went on to say, "Your Letter of Marque is a worthless piece of paper in Cuban waters. You'll be violating their territorial waters if you enter that cove. The US government is not going to have another Bay of Pigs to deal with. Do you understand that?"

Turk pounded his fist on the side of the Phantom and yelled, "Alright, I get it! We're going home for repairs. Now if you don't mind, Storm, you and your bloody friends get off my ship so we can shove-off."

Storm signaled his men to leave. As he was pushing off in the small boat he yelled out to Turk, "Don't bullshit me, Turk. We'll be watching you."

Turk ignored his last comment. He turned to his crew saying, "Man your stations and prepare to get the Phantom under way." The crew was surprised that their Captain had given in so easily to Storm's demands.

Once back on the bridge Turk waited for all of the crew to report in from their stations. He turned to Bucko and said, "Mate, plot a new course for Bermuda, and let's get this bloody ship the hell out of here."

Bucko set the coordinates and said, "Captain, the ship is yours."

Turk slammed the throttle to full power and left the Coast Guard ship in her wake. Twenty minutes later Turk turned to Bucko and said, "Bucko, plot a course for Cuba. We're going to pay MÁXIMO and his thugs a visit after all."

Bucko replied, "Roger that, Captain, but isn't Storm just going to intercept us?"

Turk laughed and said, "I know he's tracking us right now, but I've put a great deal of distance between us. That old Coast Guard cutter has no long range rockets on her to hit us from this distance. And now even if they were to try to cut us off they'd never catch up to us. We can out run her at half speed if we wanted to."

Bucko keyed in the coordinates saying, "Lets rock and roll, Captain."

Turk gave Bucko a thumbs up and turned the Phantom around heading for Cuba. It was now almost dark, and the Coast Guard ship would have no visuals on the Phantom. They could only track her on radar.

Meanwhile back on the Coast Guard ship Storm had been informed of the abrupt course change of the Phantom. Storm stomped up to the ships bridge and yelled out, "That one-eyed pirate is heading to Cuba." He turned to the captain and asked, "Is there any chance of cutting the Phantom off?" The captain shook his head in a no gesture.

Storm punched the glass window on the ship's bridge and said, "Turk has left me no choice." He pulled out a small digital device from his pocket. It looked like a MP3 player. He keyed in a code into the device and the face of the unit popped open revealing a small red button. Storm now knew that if the Phantom was overtaken by Cuban authorities a simple push of this button would set off an explosion on board the Phantom that would vaporize the entire ship leaving no trace of her existence. The US government would never allow the Phantom to fall into Cuban hands. They would also be able to deny any espionage allegations that the Cuban government might make. Storm put the device back into his pocket and just stared out over the horizon hoping he would not have to use it.

CHAPTER 22

Guantánamo Death Trap

GUANTÁNAMO
DEATH TRAP

The silent dark cloak of night was broken by a "whoop, whoop, whoop" sound streaking across the sky. Search lights flashed on from all directions instantly revealing the jet black chopper as it flew into the hidden fortress of the drug kingpin MÁXIMO. The chopper flew low across the massive cove and sat down on a helicopter pad about fifty yards from the beach. The helicopter pad was surrounded by an eight foot high barbed wire fence. MÁXIMO was not about to take any chances with any type of commando raid from other drug lords or foreign law enforcement agencies.

Before the rotation of chopper blades had come to a halt MÁXIMO's bodyguards surrounded the chopper from outside the fence. Each of the thugs was packing an AK-47 and would not hesitate to use the weapon. The pilot stayed in the chopper while two armed men stepped out on the pad. Both men reached into the chopper pulling out Saber with a black hood covering her head. Saber's hands were in hand cuffs secured behind her back. Saber struggled as best she could, but she was clearly secured by the two huge thugs manhandling her.

The armed bodyguards allowed Saber and the two thugs to exit the helicopter pad area and were escorted through the massive compound to MÁXIMO's living quarters. The thugs dragged Saber up the main stairway to the second floor where MÁXIMO's quarters were. After a walk down a long hallway the three stopped in front of a pair of massive ten foot tall cedar doors. One of the thugs turned to the other one and said, "Amigo, knock on the door." The other thug grabbed Saber by the neck and pounded her head against the solid wood door. Saber's knees buckled, but before she could collapse to the floor he grabbed her by the collar and pulled her back up on her feet. Her black hood was now soaked in blood.

A moment later a voice behind the door said, "Bring the little lady to me." The doors flung open as the two thugs entered MÁXIMO's personal lair. The thug who had Saber by the collar flung her down on the floor at MÁXIMO's feet. MÁXIMO looked down at Saber and said, "Amigos, don't be rude. Help the lady to her feet and remove her hood. I want to see her face."

The two thugs bent over and lifted her up. Just at the same moment that one of the thugs removed the hood that covered Saber's head, she spun around and kneed him in the groin sending him crashing to the floor screaming in pain. Next she spun around in the other direction kicking the legs out from under the other thug. He hit the stone floor so hard the wind was knocked out of him. While he was gasping for air Saber stood over him and stomped her foot on his face crushing his nose causing blood to spurt profusely over his face. She turned back to MÁXIMO causing him to back step, but before Saber could do anything two of MÁXIMO's bodyguards grabbed her.

With blood running down her face, Saber screamed, "You bastards! Remove these hand cuffs, and I'll take care of you too!"

MÁXIMO stepped forward trying not to show he was a bit unnerved by Saber's aggressive moves taking out the two bounty hunters. MÁXIMO calmly lit his cigar blowing the smoke in Saber's face. He laughed and said, "The little lady is not such a lady after all. She's a tigress that can rip you to shreds." He turned to the others and yelled, "Get these two poor excuses of men out of here and feed them to the sharks." Within minutes the two bounty hunters were hauled from the room.

MÁXIMO looked at Saber saying, "Soon your cowardly friends will arrive looking for you. When they enter my little cove I will blast them from the water and will personally slit each one of their throats. What do you think of that, my pretty?"

Saber's head had been bent over. She looked up at MÁXIMO and said, "They won't come, but if they do you're a dead man."

MÁXIMO started to laugh, but his temper got the best of him. He backhanded Saber across her face and said, "I'm tired of your bad manners. Take this bitch down to the torture cell and chain her to the wall. Give her no food or water. Let her rot and die there."

The two bodyguards took Saber by the arms and left the room. MÁXIMO reached over his desk and poured himself a glass of tequila, then he walked out onto his balcony overlooking the cove. He felt revenge would soon be his.

CHAPTER 23

Stealth Attack

STEALTH ATTACK

The Phantom was closing in on Cuba which also meant that the ship was about to leave the waters of the Bermuda Triangle. Soon Turk and his crew would no longer have the protection of the Letter of Marque. They would be fair game to anyone who would deem them an enemy vessel. Storm had chosen not to report the Phantom going rogue, he was hoping for a safe return from their suicidal mission.

In was in the pre-dawn hours when the Phantom left the safe waters of the Bermuda Triangle. Turk and Bucko were on the bridge having a cup of Squid's overpowering coffee.

Turk took his first sip and said, "Holy crap! Squid's coffee gets worse every day."

Bucko replied, "That's the problem, Captain. He keeps using the same old nasty coffee grinds. At least the kick it has gets you going in the morning."

Turk agreed and went on to say, "Bucko, plot a course today that will keep us away from the Cuban shores. I don't want to draw any attention to our craft on Cuban radar. By tonight we'll be around to the southern side of the island."

Bucko replied, "Roger that, Captain, but what about the Americans at the Guantanamo Bay Naval base? Don't you think they'll have a fix on us?"

Turk replied, "Bloody hell, don't you think Agent Storm has already told them we're on our way?"

Bucko agreed, "I suppose you're right, Captain."

Both men could not be more wrong. Storm had elected to remain silent. If the US Navy believed they were under attack, an immediate and deadly airstrike would be called up. There would be no way the Phantom would survive such an attack. However, if the base assumed it was a Cuban patrol boat, they would probably be left alone. No matter what was going to happen, Turk and his crew on the Phantom were going to attempt a dangerous rescue of Saber.

The Phantom arrived off Cuba's southern shores shortly after a blanket of darkness had settled over Cuba. Turk stood on the deck surveying the southern coast with his monocular. After a few minutes he turned back to Bucko who was still in the bridge and yelled out, "Bucko, call all hands on deck." Bucko did as he was told. Very quickly Dawg, Squid and Mulate joined Turk and Bucko on the deck.

Bucko looked over at a distracted Turk saying, "Captain, all present. What's the plan of attack?"

Turk paused for a minute; he could not let his thoughts of Saber go. He was hoping that MÁXIMO had not already brought harm to her. Finally Turk turned to his men and said, "Mates, tonight there will be no friends, only foes. We will be walking into a trap that MÁXIMO has ready waiting for us. They will be expecting the Phantom to try to sneak into the cove under stealth mode or an all out attack with guns blazing."

Dawg added, "I prefer the cowboy option. Let's get it on and go kick some Cuban ass."

Bucko interrupted saying, "You heard the Captain; they're probably expecting that. We'll be sunk before we can make it to shore."

Turk added, "We can debate this all night so I choose option three."

Squid ask, "What the hell is option three?"

Turk smiled and said, "Dawg, Squid, Igor and I are going to sail our dinghy straight into the cove and find a safe place to land. No one's radar will pick us up, and with no engine sounds we will not be detected from the shore. After that we'll move through the jungle to the main compound and find Saber. All the while we'll also be setting explosive charges to blow this drug lord and his lair to hell."

Bucko asked, "Aren't you taking a chance having Igor with you? What if he starts barking?"

Turk replied, "He's going to be our fear factor. I'm going to paint him up just a bit. Believe me if any drug smuggler sees him on a dead run, they'll be screaming and running for their lives." Turk continued saying, "Once we have Saber we'll blow up everything we can on our way to the shoreline. At some point I'll fire off a blue flare and that will be your signal to blast your way into the cove. You take out anything you see that moves, except for us. When we get aboard it's anyone's guess as to what happens next." Turk paused for a moment and then added, "Any questions?"

Mulate added, "Well, mon, I'll give it to you. It's one hell of a plan. Now don't take me wrong because I'm in, but most of us might never make it back to the waters of the Bermuda Triangle."

Turk replied, "Thanks for the vote of confidence, mate. You may be right, but we're going to give those bastards one hell of a run for their money." Turk looked over at Squid and said, "Come on, mate, let's go lower that dinghy into the water and set sail."

Dawg spoke up saying, "Captain, you go get Igor, and I'll help Squid."

Turk went below to get Igor while Dawg and Squid took care of the dinghy. Mulate and Bucko also went below to gather up the automatic weapons and explosives the team would need.

Meanwhile back at the lair, all was quiet. Sentries were posted down on the beach and stationed around the compound. MÁXIMO was feeling quite confident that whenever the Phantom showed up he would finally eliminate the cowards who had cost him millions of dollars of drug sales and profits. He would gladly slit the throats of any of these cowards if he had a chance to.

Below ground in her damp, dirty holding cell, Saber was sitting on the stone floor with her hands chained to an iron ring above her head. She could see old blood stains on the floor and the walls. This cell must have been used as a torture cell for MÁXIMO's rivals. Saber was on the verge of passing out, but the rats crawling over her feet kept her from losing consciousness. With no guards posted to watch her she knew that they did not fear her escaping and had left her to die. She also knew that without a rescue, escape was hopeless. Saber kicked at the rats trying to keep them at bay, but she knew deep inside that she could not survive in this environment much longer.

A few minutes later, to her surprise, the small peek-hole door opened. Saber could see an eye staring at her. She had a bad feeling about what was going to happen next. A voice from the other side of the door said, "My lovely, can I make you more comfortable?" Saber acted like she did not hear the voice in hope that the man would go away. The man on the other side of the door tried again saying, "I can get you out of here."

Saber finally replied, "You bastard, just leave me alone."

The door flung open; it was one of the bodyguards. He was a big man. All Saber could think about after seeing his face was that he must have been involved in the losing side of a lot of fights. Boy, was his face scarred. The bodyguard walked over to Saber and bent down to where his face was within inches of hers. He looked into her eyes and said, "It's time for a kiss." He reached down and grabbed Saber's shoulders and started to lift her up off the floor.

Saber screamed out, "You dumb ass, you can kiss my wall."

The bodyguard was startled, but before he could react Saber wrapped her legs around his bloated mid-section. With all her might she picked him up and slammed his head against the wall. He never knew what hit him. Saber flipped his limp body off to her left. Now all she had to do was to extract the cuff keys from his pocket. With her hands chained above her she could only use her feet to get the keys. It took her awhile, but she finally kicked her shoes off. Then with her toes she tried to get the keys out of the big lug's pocket.

Back on the Phantom the dinghy had been loaded with weapons and explosives. Squid and Dawg were in the dinghy which had already been lowered down to the water. Dawg yelled up to the boat, "Where the hell is Turk? We don't have all night."

Turk yelled back, "We're coming. Don't be so bloody impatient." Before Turk got to the edge of the Phantom, a large black creature jumped over the side and landed squarely in the middle of the dinghy between Squid and Dawg. Both men started yelling and just about jumped out of the boat. Then all of a sudden the monster creature started licking the two of them in their faces.

Dawg yelled out, "It's you, Igor! You scared the crap out of me." Squid still didn't say a word; he just hugged Igor.

Turk laughed as he climbed down into the dinghy. He then said, "Sorry mates, I didn't mean to scare the hell out of you; but since I did, I guess I did a good job fixing up Igor." Turk had spray painted Igor jet black leaving a few unpainted places on him that looked like silver streaks. He also used a bright blood- red glowing paint around his mouth area with red markings down his front legs and a skull on his chest.

Bucko laughed saying, "Captain, that poor dog in the dark of night will be confused for a demon from hell."

Turk smiled and replied, "You got that right. Now let's shove off, mates." While they were sailing away from the Phantom, Turk turned back and said in a low voice, "Lock and load, mates. Don't let us down." A minute later the dinghy sailed into the black of night and was gone.

Bucko turned to Mulate and said, "You heard the Captain. Even though there's only two of us, let's load up every weapon on the Phantom and be ready to fire everything we've got."

Mulate replied, "The Phantom's going to be one hell of a deadly fireworks display." The two went on about their business. They knew that time was short and they would have to be ready the second they saw the blue flare in the night sky.

CHAPTER 24

All Hell Breaks Loose

ALL HELL BREAKS LOOSE

The dinghy was now in the center of the cove and had remained undetected by the drug smugglers. The three men never said a word. Even Igor appeared to be content lying down asleep in the floor of the dinghy. Turk began using hand signals pointing in the direction where he wanted Squid to steer the dinghy for a landing. From about one hundred yards out Dawg lowered the sail, and the dinghy floated in with the waves to the sandy shore. Once on the beach Dawg and Turk pulled the dinghy up into the jungle while Squid kept watch for the sentries and also covered up the tracks they had made in the sand.

Out of nowhere a voice yelled out, "Who goes there, amigo?" Squid had missed spotting one of the sentries just walking onto the beach. Squid froze in his tracks not saying a work. Turk had remained hidden in the jungle watching as the sentry walked closer to Squid with his AK-47 pointed in his direction.

Turk bent down to Igor and yelled, "Get the squirrel." Just like any dog hearing "get the squirrel" it was like being told to charge at one hundred miles per hour. Igor jumped out of the jungle on all fours growling and charging at the sentry. The sentry jerked around seeing this large black beast with blood all over his mouth, snarling at him. He threw down his

AK-47 to run for his life, but before he could get ten feet Dawg reach out with a massive round house punch that stopped him dead in his tracks. A second later Igor ran up to the sentry and started licking him in the face. Turk and Squid dragged the man off into the jungle and hog tied him.

Turk came out of the jungle saying, "Good job!" He also gave Igor a pat on the head. Turk looked around. He could see they were not far from the main fortress compound. He looked at Squid and said, "Squid, I want you to sneak up and down the beach one hundred yards in both directions and set explosive charges for twenty minutes. Once you get that done try to find the drug warehouses and set explosives there, too. Then meet us back on the beach. By then we'll be needing your firepower."

Squid took off down the beach without a word. Turk turned to Dawg saying, "We have to find Saber and MÁXIMO, and I'll bet they're not together."

Dawg asked, "What the hell do you want with MÁXIMO? You know we're not in the business of taking prisoners."

Turk snapped back saying, "Who the bloody hell said we were taking prisoners? I'm going to kill this drug cartel by cutting the head off the snake. Dawg, you climb up the wall and check out the second floor. I'll take the main floor, but don't do anything until the explosions start going off. This place will be in total chaos when that happens." The two parted company and waited for the explosions.

Meanwhile Saber had managed to get two toes in the pocket of the body-guard. Just as she was pinching the key between her toes the big man started moaning and coming to. Saber yelled out, "Oh no you don't, you bastard." She raised her other leg and pounded it on his head as hard as she could again and again. Finally he went silent. Once she got the key out of the pocket, she swung her legs up over her head. It seemed to take an eternity, but she finally was able to insert the key into the lock. A few minutes later she was able to turn the key. With a thud her arms fell to the floor. She had been hanging so long that they were numb, and it took her a few minutes to get the feeling back. Saber grabbed the AK-47 from the back of the bodyguard. She also reached into his pockets and removed the five clips of bullets he was packing. Her first instinct was to stay where she was for awhile, but there was only one way in and one way out. Saber put her shoes back on and slowly pulled herself to her feet. She stepped carefully over the bodyguard and made her way out into the hallway. She flipped off the safety on the AK-47 and cocked the firing bolt back. There was no way these thugs were going to beat the crap out of her again. She might go down fighting, but she would take a lot of them with her. Saber crept quietly down the long hallway. Her plan was to make her way outside and hide in the jungle.

Turk and Igor had made their way to the porch steps that led up to the main level. They would wait there until the explosions started. Dawg had climbed up a vine covered trellis to a balcony that he could hide on.

Squid was now placing the last of his charges in the bamboo warehouses which were full of cocaine and crack. As he went through the last warehouse he noticed ten pallets of wooden crates with the name Bermuda painted on them. He definitely wanted to destroy these crates, but he wondered what was in the crates. Squid very quietly went over to one of the crates and pried up one of the corners. The packing was so dense he could still not see what was in the crate. Squid pried the corner up more and reached deeper into the crate. When he pulled his hand out he was shocked at what he found. It was a Saturday Night Special hand gun. He pulled out more, and they were all the same. These cheaply made illegal hand guns were used by street gangs all over the world. MÁXIMO was not only involved in smuggling drugs into Bermuda; he was also smuggling firearms to Bermuda. No wonder guns were popping up all over Bermuda in the hands of gangs. Squid made sure his last three charges were going to blow the hell out of these weapons. There was no way Squid was going to let this stash of weapons enter his beloved Bermuda. Squid was done, now he needed to get back to the beach.

Squid made his way about ten yards down the path when two sentries stepped out onto the path with their AK-47s pointed directly at him. One of the sentries said, "Amigo, drop your weapon."

Squid reacted by raising his weapon, but before he could get off a shot one of the sentries shot him in the shoulder. At the same moment Squid fell down, the charges he had set all over the compound began exploding. The two sentries were shaken, but they were still walking towards Squid to finish him off. Just as they took aim the weapons warehouse begin exploding. The two sentries must have been hit fifty times by exploding bullets from the Saturday Night Specials. Although shot in the shoulder Squid knew he had to get to his feet and make it back to the beach. As he stood up he felt a terrible pain in his backside. He twisted around as much as he could only to discover he had been shot in the butt by those exploding pistols. Squid knew that if he survived this ordeal he would be the butt of all the jokes aboard the Phantom. He continued on down the trail as fast as he could limp.

Explosions were now erupting all over the compound. One would have thought that an invasion was taking place. Dawg took advantage of the explosions and broke through the two French doors on the balcony where he had been hiding. The door blew open into the room throwing glass and wood door fragments in all directions. Dawg wasted no time. Within a split second he was firing his M16 all over the room. After a few seconds he stopped firing and rolled behind a massive desk. Once the smoke had cleared he had hoped to assess his situation.

Before he could look around a voice through the smoke said, "Amigo, this is no way to enter my home." Dawg was at a loss for words. He could not believe anyone could have survived his barrage of bullets. The voice went on to say, "Drop your weapon or you will die, my friend."

Dawg had had enough. He jumped up and began firing in the direction of the voice, but before he stopped he felt something rip through his upper back. Cringing in pain Dawg turned around only to be struck in the face with a butt of a pistol. It was MÁXIMO standing in front of him pointing a pistol at him. MÁXIMO laughed and fired two more shots into Dawg. Dawg fell back and collapsed on the balcony. MÁXIMO stood over him and said, "Amigo, this is my house and you're not welcome. Just like you, your friends are dead men when I find them." He laughed assuming he had killed Dawg; then he walked back inside and went over to his desk. He picked up the phone on his desk. A few seconds later when someone on the other end of the line answered he yelled out, "I'm under attack! Get the local garrison to my home now!" He slammed down the phone and stormed out of the room.

Saber had made her way down the long hallway and was about to make her way up the stairway when she looked up to see three of MÁXIMO's men descending down the stairs at her. It was no time to hesitate. She fired off the entire clip of bullets from her weapon into the men. She sidestepped their out-of-control bodies as they tumbled down the stairs past her. Saber never looked back. She removed the spent clip from her weapon and snapped in a new one as she made her way up the stairs. She had heard the explosions and now assumed a rescue must be well under way. As she cleared the stairs to the main floor she looked around and saw a beastly creature running directly at her. In and instant she took aim, but it was too late. Before she knew what hit her she was being mauled by the beast.

Then it hit her she was being licked in the face and not bitten. Saber yelled out, "Igor, is that you?"

To her amazement a voice replied, "Yes, it is."

Saber gave Igor a hug as she stood up. She then saw Turk standing behind Igor. Turk reached over and gave her a hug. With a few tears rolling down her face, Saber said, "I thought it was all over for me."

Turk looked at her and said, "You look like you've had a rough go of it".

Saber snapped back, "Thanks a lot."

Turk with a frustrated look said, "We'd better get the bloody hell out of here while we can. Follow me."

They turned and ran for the front door, but half way down the hall Turk saw it was still too heavily guarded. They turned down another hallway and found their way to the kitchen. Turk could see from there that they could make their way out into a massive courtyard. The three ran out into the courtyard only to find two sentries waiting for them.

One of the sentries yelled out, "Take one more step, and it will be your last." He looked at Igor and added, "If that beast moves an inch I'll blow his head off."

Turk reached down and grabbed Igor by the collar and said, "Not a problem, mates."

The other sentry added, "MÁXIMO will be glad to see we've captured you. Now drop your weapons."

A voice from above them said, "Not so fast. You two had better drop your weapons."

Turk turned around and looked up. It was Dawg. He was covered with blood and was leaning over the balcony. The two sentries started to fire at Dawg. Turk fired off a single shot which struck one sentry in the head and dropped him to the ground instantly. Dawg fired on the other sentry striking him in the chest. He fell over backwards into a large bush.

Turk yelled, "Dawg, stay there! I'll come up and get you."

Dawg snapped back, "Get the hell out of here. I'll catch up to you shortly." Before Turk could say anything else Dawg turned away and stumbled back into the house.

Turk knew he would never see Dawg again. He looked at Saber and said, "We need to get back to the shoreline and hook up with Squid." Saber nodded her head and they ran through the garden towards the beach.

CHAPTER 25

The Great Escape

THE GREAT ESCAPE

Back on the Phantom Bucko and Mulate were sitting on "pins and needles" waiting for the signal from Turk for the pickup.

Keeping a keen eye on the shoreline, Mulate said, "Bucko, that's one of the best fireworks displays I've ever seen."

Bucko replied, "That drug lord must be one pissed off dude about now. It looks like his entire drug operation is up in smoke."

Bucko was right. As they spoke MÁXIMO and the rest of his thugs were on their way to the beach to find and kill Turk and whoever was with him.

Turk, Saber and Igor made it to the beach. Turk checked around looking for Squid with no success. Finally he said, "I hope my little buddy made it. He definitely set the explosive charges." Turk pulled out the flare gun from his belt and fired off the blue flare which streaked across the night sky.

Out of the darkness Squid stepped out of the jungle and said, "It's about time you made it. I was beginning to worry." Squid looked around and asked, "Where's my mate Dawg?"

Turk shook his head and replied, "I'm afraid our good friend didn't make it."

Saber walked over to Squid and said, "You look worse than I do."

Squid replied, "Yeah, but you should see those other guys."

Turk interrupted by saying, "I hate to break up this reunion, but keep a look out. I'm sure MÁXIMO will be here soon."

Meanwhile Bucko and Mulate had seen the signal rocket across the night sky. The Phantom was now on a high speed run for the beach to pickup Turk, Saber, Squid and Igor. Mulate was stationed at the Gatling gun and had the depth charge firing remote with him. Bucko would be able to fire off heat seeking missiles if needed. Bucko was not trying to hide anything. He even had all of the search lights focused on the beach so he could find his friends quickly. As the Phantom raced closer to the shoreline, she came under fire from the shore. The sentries that were left were firing everything they had at the Phantom.

Saber was the first from the shoreline to get a glimpse of the Phantom. She yelled out, "Boys, get ready for a pickup." They all started backing out into the water.

Turk looked at the other two and pointed towards the jungle as he said, "Start laying out a line of fire into the jungle. I'm sure these thugs will be showing up before the Phantom does." Turk was right, MÁXIMO and his thugs were only seconds away.

As Turk looked over his shoulder checking on the Phantom he felt a excruciating pain rip through his right thigh. He dropped down in the water grabbing at his leg. Saber reached over and helped him back to his feet with one arm while she was still firing with the other arm.

Back on the Phantom Bucko yelled out to Mulate, "In a couple of minutes I'll be spinning the Phantom around just short of the beach. Otherwise if we get too close to the shore we'll get beached. When I spin around it's up to you to protect Turk and the others and get them onboard."

Mulate yelled back, "Roger that, mon."

Squid could now see that the pickup was almost at hand. He turned to the others and said, "Let's get moving. We're too close to the shoreline to get picked up."

Saber and Turk turned towards the open water and kept firing over their shoulders. MÁXIMO and his thugs were now on the beach firing at the Phantom's crew as they tried to escape.

MÁXIMO yelled out, "Kill them."

As the bullets pierced the air around Turk and his crew, the Phantom was almost on top of them.

Bucko yelled out, "Let her rip!" As the Phantom roared up to the beach he cut the power and made a one eighty turn to the starboard. The Phantom threw a massive wave on the beach almost washing MÁXIMO and his thugs back into the jungle. Unfornatunately Turk and the crew were also washed back towards the shore.

Mulate laid down a heavy line of fire on the beach. Then he quickly ran to the bow of the Phantom and threw out four life preservers with lines tied to the boat. He yelled out, "Grab the life preservers and hold on."

Squid and Igor were first to get to the life preservers. Saber was half way to her preserver when she noticed Turk was struggling to get back to his feet. As he stood up he was tackled from behind by two of MÁXIMO's thugs. Saber started to head back to Turk, but Squid grabbed her and pulled her back to the preserver.

Saber screamed out, "Let me go! We've got to save Turk!"

Squid in a reassuring voice replied, "We can help him more on the Phantom than here in the water."

Saber was pulled onboard first. Because Squid had his arms wrapped around Igor it took both Mulate and Bucko to pull them onboard.

Meanwhile the two thugs dragged Turk up on the beach to MÁXIMO. All the crew of the Phantom could do was watch. Mulate took his position back at the Gatling gun while the others continued to watch. In a low tone Mulate said, "Bucko, give me thirty seconds and I'll put an end to these bloody devils. Then we'll get Turk back."

Bucko replied, "Not in the cards, mate. One wild shot and our Captain will be dead." Bucko was already thinking to himself that Turk was probably not going to survive no matter what they did.

While the Phantom's crew was forced into a stalemate MÁXIMO walked up to Turk and said, "So this is the captain of the marauders who have cost me millions of dollars."

Turk looked straight into his eyes and said, "Bite me, mate."

Enraged MÁXIMO pulled out a switch blade from his pocket and flipped it open. Turk could see the stone cold look in his eyes and expected the worse. MÁXIMO took the double edged knife and shoved it into Turks side and twisted it. Turk bent over in agony. MÁXIMO removed the knife from Turks body and casually wiped the blood from his knife on Turks shirt. MÁXIMO smiled and whispered into Turk's ear, "Not to worry, amigo. I won't kill you for awhile. If I did, your friends with all their firepower would kill us in a few seconds. If I keep you alive a little while longer, your friends will be doomed. The Cuban navy will be here soon and blow that boat to kingdom come."

Watching from the Phantom, Saber screamed out, "They're killing him!"

Mulate yelled, "Just one shot!"

Before anyone on the Phantom could do anything, automatic weapon fire ripped through the dense jungle. One by one each of MÁXIMO's thugs begin dropping to the beach like flies. As the last thug dropped MÁXIMO could see a figure stepping out of the jungle. He quickly grabbed Turk and spun him around and stuck his knife to his throat. He yelled out, "Drop your weapon, or I will slit your friend's throat!"

The voice yelled back, "Who gives a damn?"

Turk could now see the figure. To his disbelief it was good old Dawg. He had thought he was dead; in fact, he did look half dead right now.

Dawg looked back at Turk and said, "Captain, I don't know which one of us looks the worse for wear." Dawg paused for a few seconds almost falling over in severe pain.

Before Dawg could continue MÁXIMO interrupted him saying, "Amigo, back off. Since you missed shooting me, I still hold the power right now."

Dawg laughed, "You dumb bastard! I never shot at you. I was just leveling the playing field for Turk. Now it's one on one."

MÁXIMO looked bewildered for a moment, but that was all the time Turk needed. Turk grabbed MÁXIMO's hand that was holding the knife and snapped it back as hard as he could. Turk could hear bones breaking in MÁXIMO's hand. The knife went flying and Turk wasted no time nailing him in the jaw with a round house right. MÁXIMO stumbled backwards and fell over the bodies of two of his dead thugs. He quickly grabbed one of their AK-47's and fired a shot that grazed Turk's forehead. He took aim at Turk again and another shot rang out. Turk stumbled back, but he couldn't tell where he was hit. He looked over at MÁXIMO only to see his eyes rolling back into his head. MÁXIMO dropped to his knees and fell face down in the sand. Turk looked back at Dawg, but he was in no condition to shoot anyone else right now. In fact he was using his M16 as a crutch just to hold him up.

Back on the Phantom Turk heard a voice yell out, "Mon, as I said before, just one shot." Mulate had taken the opportunistic shot at MÁXIMO just at the right moment.

Turk staggered over to Dawg and lifted his other arm over his shoulder saying, "Dawg, I think it's time we get the hell out of here before all hell breaks loose."

Dawg smiled and added, "You think?" Both men slowly made their way into the water. Squid and Saber had already jumped back into the water to help Turk and Dawg as they made their way out to the Phantom.

As they approached the Phantom Bucko yelled out, "You bloody better hurry it up. An armed Cuban patrol boat just entered the cove."

As the four climbed onboard Turk yelled out to Bucko, "Just for good measure fire a few rockets into the compound."

Bucko replied, "Roger that Captain." Bucko fired off three heat seeking missiles directly into the main compound. The explosions were immediate and massive. MÁXIMO, his compound, and his drug network were now totally destroyed.

Turk looked at the crew and added, "Tonight we took a huge bite out of the drug world. Now we still have the Cuba Navy to deal with. And who knows maybe we can get back home." Turk thought to himself, "Getting through the Cubans and making it to the open sea was one big bloody if."

CHAPTER 26

Every Which Way But

Out

EVERY WHICH WAY BUT OUT

A Cuban patrol boat had in fact just entered MÁXIMO's private cove. After seeing the compound exploding and burning, the commander called for additional support. At this point the Cuban commander had no idea if this was a US raid from the Guantanamo Bay Naval Base or an execution style attack from another drug cartel. No matter what, he was not going to take any chances. As the Cuban patrol boat closed in on the beach the commander spotted the Phantom. He had never seen a vessel like this before. The sleek design of the Phantom was puzzling to him. Was it a war ship or a drug smuggler's ship? This was no time for indecision. The commander ordered his crew to blast the ship out of the water. The patrol boat opened fire with mounted machine guns on the deck and small cannon fire as it raced towards the Phantom.

Turk had been hesitant to open fire on the Cubans. He was not at war with them, but after being fired upon he knew the Cubans meant business and the closer they drew the more their lives were in danger. Turk was not about to surrender. The thought of spending the rest of his life in a Cuban prison was not acceptable. Finally he yelled out, "Battle stations, defend your positions." He took over control of the bridge while Bucko took over the rocket and depth charge station. Mulate stayed on the Gatling gun, and

Squid picked up a grenade launcher. Saber grabbed her pistol and strapped on a first aid kit just in case the others were hit by Cuban fire. Seeing everyone was in position, Turk picked up the ship's microphone and said, "Fire at will, mates. It's kick ass time, and we're not stopping for anyone." Turk threw the ship's throttle wide opened and yelled out, "Geronimo!" The Phantom lunged forward for a split second and then threw out a wake thirty feet high as she maxed out to full speed in ten seconds.

Mulate had already begun firing his Gatling gun in rapid succession. Even at a distance his bullets were ripping holes through the Cuban patrol boat. The two ships were now both on a direct hit collision course and both were taking hits from each other. The Cuban commander now knew he was in a dog fight with a well armed opponent. Making it worse the Phantom was bigger and traveling at three times the speed he was. He quickly unleashed one hundred percent of his fire power at the Phantom. Because of the Phantom's speed most of his cannon shots missed and what few did hit seemed to bounce off the angled sides of the Phantom.

Turk looked over at Bucko and yelled, "Fire a heat seeker at those bastards and see how they like that."

Bucko replied, "Roger that, Captain. Locked and loaded." Bucko quickly locked onto the patrol boat and fired off the heat seeker.

Even in the darkness the Cuban commander could see the missile was going to make a direct hit on his boat. He made a turn at full throttle to his starboard to avoid the heat seeker and then fired off a flare gun to draw the missile away. His plan worked; the missile hit the flair and exploded about twenty yards from his boat. His brief moment of relief turned in to horror a second later.

The Phantom was almost on top of the patrol boat. Turk yelled out, "Hold on, mates. It's going to be one hell of a collision." A second later the Phantom broadsided the patrol boat on her port side. As the Phantom sliced through the boat it exploded into a million pieces. The only thing left in the wake of the Phantom was burning floating debris.

Squid looked back and said, "Captain, the Cuban military is going to be pissed off at us."

That's what Turk was afraid of. They had just blasted their way out of the cove by blowing up a Cuban patrol boat. There was not going to be any safe refuge anywhere. He knew that the Guantanamo Bay Naval Base would disavow any knowledge of the Phantom and make no offer of safe harbour. Turk would have to decide quickly if they would try to outrun the Cuban Navy or to move out in stealth at a slower speed and hope by morning they would be out of Cuban waters. Turk turned to the crew and asked, "Well mates, what will it be? Are we going to run and gun or sneak out?"

It was unanimous. The crew voted to "run and gun."

Turk added, "Mates, there's no stopping now until we hit international waters. I just hope if we get that far the Cubans realize it too." Turk went on to say, "Tend to your wounds and have a beer and relax. Shortly we're going to be hit from all directions, sea and air." Turk turned back to the ship's wheel and threw the throttle forward and just stared across the horizon as the Phantom made its way for the waters of the Bermuda Triangle. Saber came up from behind him and wrapped one of her arms around him. Nothing was said. They both just stood there like it was meant to be. Finally Saber let go. She needed to go and help patch up the rest of the crew's wounds. As the Phantom raced across the calm black waters of the Caribbean, the crew was silent. They had always been the hunters; now they were the hunted.

CHAPTER 27

The Bermuda Triangle
or Bust

THE BERMUDA TRIANGLE OR BUST

In the early predawn hours the Phantom which was not running in stealth mode was surly being tracked by Cuban radar. Turk and Bucko were still on the bridge. Bucko walked over to Turk saying, "Captain, how about a fresh brew?"

Turk turned to Bucko taking the coffee and replied, "Thanks, mate." He then added, "Check out the radar and see if we're being followed. Also check the bloody GPS and see how far we are from breaking around the tip of this big ass island."

Bucko checked both screens and replied, "It's still all clear, and it's another fifty kilometers before we have a straight shot at the waters of the Bermuda Triangle."

Turk added, "Thanks, mate. Go tell the rest of the crew to be ready to man their stations in less than an hour. All hell will be breaking loose soon."

Bucko replied, "Aye, Captain." He quickly left the bridge to alert the others.

Turk had been right about the Cuban authorities who had been tracking the Phantom all night. Not knowing who they were tracking they were hesitant to attack the fleeing vessel. After watching the course of the Phantom they had pretty much eliminated the possibility of a commando raid from the Guantanamo Bay Naval Base. The ship was making a run for it in the opposite direction of Guantanamo Bay. It would be light soon, and they would make their decision then. Until then they would watch and wait.

The Cubans were not the only ones watching the events over the last several hours. Derrick Storm had made his way to the Guantanamo Bay Naval Base overnight and was also tracking the Phantom. Now that the drug lord MÁXIMO and his entire operation was destroyed Storm updated the Commander of the base as to the events that had taken place over the last twenty-four hours.

Storm finished by asking the base commander, "Is there anything you can do to protect the Phantom?"

The commander replied, "Right now there is an unknown craft in Cuban waters that does not even exist in the eyes of the United States Government. There is no way in hell I'm going to intervene and cause a Cuban military crisis. Why in the hell aren't they running in stealth mode anyway?"

Storm snapped back, "The Phantom can run at twice the speed when it's not in stealth mode. I'm sure Turk knew he could never clear Cuban waters before daylight in stealth mode; so they had to make a run for it."

The commander shook his head and said, "Right now my hands are tied. The Phantom is still in Cuban waters."

Storm slammed his fist down on the table and yelled, "That's a crock and you know it." Storm turned away and stomped out of the room. The commander said nothing. He stood there looking down at the tracking screen and scratched his chin thinking about what Storm had said.

Meanwhile a local Cuban patrol who had finally reached the destroyed compound had found one of MÁXIMO's thugs barely alive. Just before he died he told them that the perpetrators were the marauders who were the ones that were destroying their drug shipments. Upon hearing this news the corrupt local Communist party leader called off the Cuban military. He had a much better plan to destroy the foreign marauders.

As the first rays of light were cast across the eastern sky, the Phantom had just made its way around the far southeastern tip of Cuba. Turk looked at the radiant sunrise and for a few seconds forgot that this spectacular sunrise just might be the kiss of death for him and his crew. A few minutes later, as the last of the morning fog was clearing Turk got the shock of his life. The Phantom was on a direct course with what looked like a small fleet of Stinger racing boats.

Turk yelled out, "All hands man your stations." Just as they did the night before, the crew scrambled back to their stations except for Saber. This time she locked up Igor below deck and grabbed a M16 with a bag full of clips.

Bucko from his station on the bridge asked, "What the hell are we heading into, a drug runners convention?"

Turk cracked a small smile and said, "It looks like the Cuban military didn't want to deal with us. They must have sent every drug smuggler, thug, and bounty hunter in Cuba after us."

Bucko looked out at the ship filled horizon and said, "There's so damn many of them. There must be at least fifty boats out there just waiting for us."

Turk added, "We'll never out run them, and we're not going back to Cuba; so if it's a battle they want then it's a battle they're going to get. One thing is for sure, Bucko my man, after today there's going to be a lot less drug smugglers and drug dealers on this earth." Turk slammed the throttle forward to the maximum and yelled out, "Mulate, send those bastards a welcome and don't stop until they've all gone home to Davy Jones." Mulate set his Gatling gun to automatic and just hung on for the ride.

The fleet of Stingers were spread out over several hundred yards and were five to six deep. It was obvious to Turk that they were going to flank both sides of the Phantom and try to surround her in a pincher maneuver. Turk was not worried about being out smarted; he was worried about being out gunned. The Stingers had twenty times the weapons that the Phantom had. Turk waited a minute and when the Stingers began to flank the Phantom on both sides he yelled out, "Bucko, fire all the torpedoes now!" Bucko fired all the Phantom's torpedoes at once—three torpedoes from the starboard side and three from the port side. Each torpedo struck a boat almost instantly. The rapid explosions caused other Stingers to lose control and crash into each other. In spite of all the explosions and chaos the Phantom stayed on course towards the main body of Stingers. At the last minute before contact Turk yelled out, "I'm going to give them my starboard. You give them all you've got." Turk downed the throttle and spun the wheel as hard as he could. The Phantom hit a Stinger so hard it went air bourn and crashed into another boat. Upon impact both boats exploded causing many of the other Stingers to veer off course. Turk threw the throttle full forward. He now had at least ten Stingers out flanked, and the ones with their stern facing the Phantom were being shattered by thousands of rounds of bullets from Mulate and the Gatling gun. Meanwhile on the starboard side of the Phantom, Bucko was launching depth charges at those Stingers. Some of the charges missed their targets, but still caused havoc with the boats. Two of the charges flew through the air and landed dead centre in two different Stingers. Both boats were incinerated instantly. Dawg was busy firing an M16 as the Stingers passed the Phantom while Squid was firing a grenade launcher. Just as Squid was about to fire a grenade, a Stinger pulled alongside the Phantom and one of the thugs on board emptied his AK-47 clip into him. Squid fell over dead. Upon impact his grenade exploded; so the entire stern of the Phantom was in flames now.

Turk yelled, "Can anyone put that bloody fire out?" Saber reached into the bridge and grabbed a fire extinguisher. Just as she made her way to the raging fire at the stern of the ship, one of the engines exploded. Saber was thrown backwards hitting her head against the steel hull of the Phantom. She was out cold on the deck with flames burning all around her. The Phantom could now barely propel herself. Turk was following a zigzag course through the water trying to avoid the massive barrage of bullets being fired at them.

Bucko was firing off every heat seeking missile and depth charge he had. This action alone had destroyed another ten to fifteen Stingers. Turk had just seen Saber on the deck with the flames moving very close to her. Turk turned to Bucko and said, "Take the wheel! I've got to go get Saber." Turk flew out of the bridge dodging bullets as he made his way to Saber. By the time he got there her pant leg was on fire. Turk quickly rolled her over putting the fire out. He then picked her up in his arms and ran for the bridge. Just as he was stepping through the door a bullet struck him in his shoulder. He stumbled and dropped to the floor, but was able to brace his fall against one of the map table legs. He laid Saber down and returned to the ship's wheel.

Bucko looked at him and asked, "Captain, are you alright?"

Turk took the wheel and replied, "Yeah, just as long as the rest of you keep firing your asses off."

Bucko was now out of heat seekers and depth chargers. He reached down and grabbed Saber's M16 and said, "Roger that, Captain," as he ran out the bridge's hatch. Wasting no time he immediately began firing at any boat in sight. The smoke was now so dense that no one could possibly see who they were shooting at any more.

The Phantom took several more hits in the stern with successive explosions. Turk now realized all the diesel engines on the Phantom were destroyed. The stealth electric turbines would be of no help; so the Phantom was now a sitting duck in the water. The Phantom's crew could only defend themselves with limited weapons. There would no longer be any evasive actions. Mulate was still firing wildly in all directions taking out any Stinger that came his way.

The situation was getting even more desperate. Dawg yelled to Turk, "Out of ammo."

Turk reached into his pocket and pulled out his last clip. With no hesitation he threw it to Dawg. Turk yelled back, "That's it, mate." He then gave Dawg a salute. Dawg returned the salute and slapped the clip into his M16. He turned and began firing at an approaching Stinger. Dawg's bullets ripped through the pilot of the Stinger. Now out of control, the boat broadsided the Phantom. The Stinger exploded upon it's collision with the Phantom. Dawg was blown through the air, and he crashe through the bridge's window. The Phantom's port side was now ripped open almost from bow to stern.

All went quiet and as the smoke cleared, Turk and Bucko joined Mulate on what was left of the bow. They were surrounded by the wreckage of burning Stinger boats. Just as the three were beginning to believe they had survived Turk looked up and saw a huge jet black unmarked gun boat closing in on the Phantom. Turk looked at his two friends and said, "Mates, this may be the end of the line, but we're going out with a bang." He slapped both of them on the back and added, "Let's do this."

Mulate started to go back to the Gatling gun; instead he suddenly stopped and turned back saying, "Turk, the barrel of the Gatling gun overheated and jammed. It's like us, cooked."

Bucko stepped forward and said, "Not a problem, mate." He reached into his pocket and pulled out a pistol. He went on to say, "If you can't stop that gun boat with this you can always use it on yourself."

The three men all laughed, then with two M16's and one pistol they went to the bow of the ship and pointed their weapons at the gun boat and waited. The gun boat was now within two hundred yards and closing. The boat fired its largest cannon at the Phantom. The projectile exploded in the water directly in front the Phantom. All three men were blown off their feet and smashed into the steel wall in front of the bridge. As they were trying to recover a loud piercing engine sound screamed over their heads followed immediately with explosions that seemed to engulf them with flames and smoke. All three men knew the end had arrived, but to their astonishment they were still alive. As they recovered they could see a huge ball of fire burning directly in front of them now. The gunboat had been destroyed.

Turk stood up and in disbelief said, "I'll be a son of a bitch." He looked to the sky and saw a US Navy F16 fighter jet circling above them." He added, " We must have made it to the bloody waters of the Bermuda Triangle after all." Turk was right. They were in the waters of the Bermuda Triangle, and yes, they were bloody. The carnage and devastation would match any naval battle scene in history.

The three helped each other to their feet. They limped back to the bridge to find Saber holding Dawg's head in her lap with Igor licking his face. Saber looked up at Turk and said, "We thought we lost the three of you when we heard the explosions." Turk bent down and gave Saber a kiss on the lips and said, "Not on your life, baby." He turned back to the others and said, "Mates, daylight's burning. Let's see if the stealth engine will fire up and get us home."

CHAPTER 28

Homeward Bound

HOMEWARD BOUND

As the crew began trying to put some of the pieces back a United States Coast Guard ship approached the Phantom and anchored fifty yards off her starboard. A voice over the ships loud speaker blared out, "Captain of the Phantom, we seek permission to come aboard."

Turk stuck his head out of the bridge hatch and cupped his hands around his mouth yelling, "Bloody hell, why not?"

A few minutes later a boat filled with Coast Guard personnel tied up to the Phantom. Over the next thirty minutes a medical staff tended to the wounds of the Phantom's crew while others put out the fires all over the ship. Turk was still trying to get the stealth engine started when a familiar figure stepped into the bridge. It was Derrick Storm. Storm shook Turk's hand and said, "Congratulations, Captain, to you and your crew. Job well done."

Turk replied, "Thanks, Storm, but I wish the rest of the crew were here right now. They'll be missed, but never forgotten."

Storm looked at Turk as he continued to fiddle with the control panel and asked, "Do really think you're going to get this ship going?"

Turk smiled and at that moment the electric turbines began humming. Turk added, "What can I say, mate?"

Storm scratched his head in disbelief and said, "Alright, you made your point. Forget the damn turbines. You and your entire crew need to be air lifted back to a base in the US for medical attention. In the mean time we'll tow the Phantom back and have her refitted."

Turk looked surprised. He thought he and the crew were going to be arrested. He said, "Does this mean we're still bloody phantom marauders?"

Storm smiled and replied, "Yes, Turk, this war on the drug lords is just beginning. The United States and the Bermuda government still desperately need your help. Inspector Savage told me this morning if I let you return to Bermuda without a job, he would kick the bloody hell out of both of us."

Turk smiled and shook Storm's hand then turned and left the bridge to find Saber waiting for him at the stern of the ship. He wrapped his arms around her and just before they kissed he said, "How about going on a romantic cruise?"

Saber smiled and whispered back, "Not on your life."

MORE NOVELS
BY R.C. FARRINGTON

Death Diamonds of Bermudez

Modern day Apartheid mercenaries from South Africa hell bent on establishing an independent Boer Nation will stop at nothing to ignite their coup d'état. Finding the Death Diamonds is the final piece of the puzzle in their diabolical scheme.

A small group of renegade Boer War soldiers imprisoned in Bermuda in the early nineteen hundreds discovered the treasures of Bermúdez, but never revealed the location. Their descendants with the most evil intentions have searched for the Death Diamonds of the lost city of Bermúdez to this day.

Special FBI Agent Derrick Storm and Bermuda Inspector Ian Savage are the only ones who have any chance of keeping these ruthless mercenaries from fulfilling their diabolical scheme. Out gunned and out manned Savage and Storm must rely on their gut instincts to outwit these killers.

The Spinners (from the Spinners Trilogy) find themselves drawn into a treasure hunt cloaked with deceit and deception. Somehow Savage, Storm and the Spinners must find the Death Diamonds first and prevent a nightmare of death and destruction.

217

Awards:

"Death Diamonds of Bermudez" was awarded the Shreveport – Bossier regional 2009 Silver ADDY award.

The Isle of Devils Holy War

The most explosive terrorist plot in history is about to become a reality. A secret terrorist organization has used the Western world's greed for oil to cloak their Holy War. Undercover agents try to expose the terrorists' plot on the island of Bermuda before thousands of innocent lives are in jeopardy.

FBI agent Derrick Storm from the US with the assistance of Ian Savage a Police Inspector from Bermuda attempt to uncover the most sophisticated and deadly terrorist plot ever set in motion. FBI Agent Storm is one of the top law enforcement specialists in the United States. He has a great respect for the law but will bend the rules if necessary to apprehend criminals.

Inspector Savage has a "school of hard knocks" law enforcement degree. By Bermuda police standards his actions are often unorthodox. In spite of that, he's one of the most effective crime fighters in Bermuda.

Somehow these two agents from different races, backgrounds, and countries must work together to derail the terrorist plot that grows as a serious threat to the security of the world.

Awards:

"The Isle of Devil's Holy War" was awarded the Shreveport – Bossier regional 2008 Gold ADDY award.

Spinners The Lost Treasure of Bermuda – Episode I

Episode I Five teenagers unlock the secrets of the Bermuda Triangle where the past and the present collide. "The Lost Treasure of Bermuda" has intrigued and eluded treasure hunters for more than 200 hundred years.

The Spinners have to face and survive evil villains in Bermuda and in the Bermuda Triangle who will stop at nothing to control the "Tucker Cross" and "The Lost Treasure".

Spinners The Protectors of the Bermuda Triangle – Episode II

Five teenagers from Bermuda are trapped in the Bermuda Triangle. They must face the forces of evil to protect the Triangle from destruction. Scarzo, a modern day mercenary from Brazil, kidnaps the Spinners determined to force them to reveal the secret gateway to the Bermuda Triangle. The Spinners also have the bad fortune of crossing paths with Scorpion, a Voodoo pirate from Haiti. She will stop at nothing to find the power source that controls the Bermuda Triangle.

Spinners The Curse of the Bermuda Abyss – Episode III

Five teenagers trapped in the Bermuda Triangle find themselves being drawn into the dark depths of the Bermuda Abyss. In this third episode the Spinners may have finally met their match facing the most vicious and most notorious evil being of all time. In a race for their lives and with very little time the Spinners must escape from the depths of the Bermuda Abyss and its curse.

Made in the USA
Charleston, SC
25 March 2012